Seduce Me

Georgia Le Carre

Cover design: http://www.bookcoverbydesign.co.uk/

Editor: http://www.loriheaford.com/
Proofreader:
http://nicolarhead.wix.com/proofreadingservices

Seduce Me

(Book 4 of The Billionaire Banker series)

Published by Georgia Le Carre
Copyright © 2014 by Georgia Le Carre

ISBN: 978-0-9928249-8-3

You can discover more information about Georgia Le Carre and future releases here.

https://www.facebook.com/georgia.lecarre
https://twitter.com/georgiaLeCarre
http://www.goodreads.com/GeorgiaLeCarre

Contents

Blake Law Barrington

I rub my hand down my cheeks and chin, and return the shaver to its holder. In the mirror there is nothing but me. The way I came into this world. Naked. For an instant I frown at myself. Last night I dreamed again. Of that time when my hands were small and covered in blood. I try to recall the details, but the dream is gone.

No, not gone. Of course not. It never goes. It hides inside a faint net of tension.

I turn away from my reflection and that feeling that something inside is broken and awkward, and walk into the shower. I close the door and, standing out of the trajectory of the spray, turn the knob. It comes powerfully alive. I let the water heat up before I step into the hot cascade. It sluices over me. The water is sensuous and forgiving.

I close my eyes and the water washes away my sins.

There is a small knock on the door.

I turn around and open the door. For a moment we simply look at each other. Her hair is loose about her shoulders and tousled. There are faint lines on her upper arms made by the creases in the sheets. Otherwise she is perfect. She steps inside and I open my arms to envelop her.

God, I love this woman.

She pours liquid soap into the palm of her hand and smears the soap across her breasts.

'You're asking for it,' I tell her.

'Since the day I met you,' she says softly.

I smile.

She smiles back. In the clouds of steam around us, her eyes are dark. They move slowly down my body and come to rest on my cock. It is hard and ready for her.

I spin her around. She lands neatly on the frosted glass, on her hands and elbows. Her cheek presses into the glass and her hips tilt up to receive me. I plunge into her. She gasps. I love that involuntary sound. I always ram her harder than necessary just to hear that sound. The sound is the beginning and the end of my possession of her. That's my sound. I own it. The day she stops making that sound something inside me will die.

Our wet bodies make aggressive slapping sounds as I fuck her hard and fast. The need to go deeper and deeper into her makes me lift her clean off the floor. I travel faster and faster into her silky tightness until I explode deep inside her.

When I turn her around we stare at each other, both of us panting hard. Then I get to my haunches and pulling apart her pussy lips suck her clit quite cruelly while I watch her writhing and moaning helplessly. I'm good at this and she comes quickly with a high-pitched cry. I stand and guide her back into the middle of the water.

As the water pours over us I kiss her. Her mouth is sweet and warm. For a while I lose myself in the sweetness of that kiss. Then she is moving away. I grab her hand.

'He has great timing that son of yours,' she says with a laugh, and opening the door slips out. I listen, but don't hear anything other than the towel being pulled off the rail, and her footfalls as she leaves the bathroom.

A mother's ears are special.

I turn off the tap and reach for a towel. I dry myself briskly and pad over to the adjoining room. Sometimes, Lana will bring Sorab into the dressing room while I dress. That day she doesn't. My clothes are already laid out and a pair of socks lovingly hung on the radiator. They are warm enough to heat even a heart as frozen as mine. I pull them on quickly.

I have an early appointment with India Jane, the wedding organizer. I told Lana that I didn't want her to get involved in the planning for the wedding because I didn't want her to have the crazy stress that brides go through, but that is only partly true. The real truth is I want it to be the kind of wedding that Lana would never organize for herself, not only because she doesn't know how to—her upbringing means she cannot even begin to comprehend the kind of ostentatious extravagance I have in mind—but also because one needs to be super spoilt to want

something like that for oneself. And Lana simply isn't.

Unknown to her, her wedding is going to be the biggest society event of the year. Invitations are going to be rare and precious. Not because I want it—I'd marry Lana in a bathtub tomorrow, and not give a shit—but because I know the knives are out for her. Anything less than a massive wedding will diminish her in their eyes. And she doesn't need that. Those patronizing harpies could oppress you in their sleep. But I'll get every one of those stuck-up bitches to accept her as their equal if it is the last fucking thing I do.

And to that effect even my mother is not being invited.

Yeah, she is pissed off, but she'll get over it. It may sound drastic to you, but you don't know my mother. She has the ability to ruin the entire wedding with one carefully chosen word! She can throw you a line and a hand grenade at the same time. I don't want to be decoding the nuances of her barbs.

Besides, there is no real point to inviting her: I already know exactly what her relationship with Lana is going to be like. I imagine her well-groomed hands folded in her lap, her face bathed in a wry smile as she nimbly laces Lana into a narrow relationship of superior and inferior. And from that submissive position Lana will never again be allowed to move away.

So: she's not coming. And for that matter neither is Marcus. Their absence more than

anything else will demonstrate to the rest of them that if they are planning on taking sides or sucking up to anyone it had better be to Lana.

I shrug on my jacket.

Here's the deal:

I know Lana wants me to give you my version of the events, but honestly, do you really want to hear about a wedding from a man's point of view? Weddings are for girls. The minute India Jane starts moving her jaw from her usual English expression of subdued agony and starts discussing matching boutonnières my eyes start glazing over.

The next best person would be Billie, but what she thinks of weddings and the people who indulge in them doesn't bear repeating, so, we are left with the other bridesmaid, Julie Sugar. I have only seen her once, very briefly, so I can't say I know her, but Lana grew up with and speaks very highly of her, and I trust Lana's instincts, so I'm going to leave it with her.

I understand that you don't know her, but you've bought the ticket for the show and you might as well go in with an open mind. You never know—you might enjoy it.

Master Sorab Barrington requests the pleasure of your company
at the wedding and reception of his parents

Lana Bloom

and

Blake Law Barrington

at the Old Church, Woburn, Bedfordshire on Sunday 18th May 2014 at 2.00 p.m.
followed by a reception at Wardown Towers.

A reply is requested to:
India James Pennington
Buckingham Palace Road,
London SW1 1AA

Dress:
Uniform, morning coat
or lounge suit

One

Julie Sugar

Yes, it is true: I hate Lana Bloom.

But it is also true that I agreed to be her bridesmaid.

The why of why I agreed to play bridesmaid is startlingly simple—she has something I want. The why of why I hate her is not too complicated either. It began as envy, many years ago. You see, she was everything I was not and wanted to be.

As a child her perfection and beauty had to be seen to be believed—straight black hair and the biggest, most innocent blue eyes you ever saw, while I was an ugly, ungainly thing topped with a bizarre mop of curls. She was perfectly formed and I was... Well, my nickname used to be Fatty, and when they were being kind, Fatso.

I had no drama. Drama followed her like a well-trained pet. Her mother was always dying, but never did. Her father went to work one day and never came back. A pedophile tried to snatch her. Drama, drama, drama. It was never-ending.

Oh, and I should add, Billie Black, the coolest girl in school and the one person I was dying to befriend, became her best friend. But, I guess, my real hatred for her began when—

'Julie,' my mother bellows from downstairs.

'What?' I yell back.

'I got you a donut.'

'I'll come and get it,' I shout, quickly scampering off my bed and landing on the floor with a soft thud. I hear her heavy tread pass into the living room. I unlock my door, run down the stairs and stand at the foot of them. From this vantage point I have a view of the kitchen and the living room.

On the kitchen table I can see the thin, white paper bag with the donut in it. In the living room I see a woman. A huge woman. The last time she weighed herself she was nearing four hundred pounds. That was nearly a year ago.

She looks like a mountain of lard held together by a thin layer of human skin, pasty white and stretched so tight you can see all her veins, green and working themselves to death to service the large needs of her body. She collapses backwards into the sofa. The springs are gone but three cushions squash obediently into the shape of her massive arse.

Under her tent-like, gray T-shirt she wears no bra, and two broad flattened pieces of flesh lay over her stomach. Where the shapeless T-shirt ends her meaty elbows begin. They bloom into club like hands that clumsily fan out into fat red sausage-like fingers. The sausages are clutching a greasy paper bag that she brings up to her chest. Her hands do not reach higher. Her neck bends and she buries her face in the first Jamaican pattie of the three she will have bought: they supersize them especially for her at the bakery down the road.

She is my mother.

She lifts her head—her lips are covered with a coating of greasy brown gravy and her mouth is so full, her cheeks bulge. She chews exactly three times and swallows. 'It's in the kitchen,' she says.

'Yeah, I see it. Thanks,' I say, but do not move.

She nods, bites off another chunk of pastry and returns her gaze to the TV screen. Next, she will reach for the two liter bottle of Coke and guzzle from it. She goes through a bottle a day. Not taking her eyes off the TV she stretches for the bottle.

I go into the kitchen. The place is an unbelievable pigsty. There are many days worth of dirty dishes to be done and a coating of grease and grime everywhere. The cooker is so encrusted with spills, stains, and dirt that there is not a speck of white left on it. The linoleum floor is thick with crud and the dustbin is in need of emptying. It stinks.

I stop breathing.

When I was younger I used to come home from school and clean, but as if my mother and brother

9

prefer to live in filth it was almost impossible to keep the grime and dirt away. I stopped when my brother acquired a dog.

Then it became impossible.

It is exactly like one of those homes on that *How Clean Is Your House TV* series where those two busybody expert cleaners, Kim and Aggie, go to really dirty houses to help clean them. Sometimes I watch the show just to see if I can find a home dirtier than ours. Once they had this woman on who had, like, fifty cats living in her basement flat and that was real bad, worse than our flat.

I snatch the paper bag off the table and, without touching anything else, run up the stairs. I close and lock my door and look around the room. Shades of pink, neat and scrupulously, scrupulously clean.

I take a deep breath, let the scent of green apples filtering out of the air freshener plug-in fill my lungs, before I go to my bedside drawer. I find a plate and put it on top of the bedside cabinet. Then I take the donut out of the paper bag. Jam donuts are my most favorite thing in the whole wide world. When I was a kid I could eat a whole Sainsbury's packet of six in one sitting.

I lay the paper bag on the plate and the donut on top of it. Then I sit on the bed and look at it. At the sugar-dusted layer and the lovely reddened bit where you can see where they have piped in the jam. I think of it in my mouth. The rough grains of sugar, the thin fried skin, the deliciously doughy bit beneath, and finally, the sticky squirt of sweet jam on my tongue. Saliva fills my mouth.

I swallow hard. I remember my science teacher once said that the desire to eat is instinctive, a mechanism of evolution. A newborn babe knows to turn its head towards a nipple. Without food the species would die.

A shiver passes through my body.

I open the bedside drawer and from a box of disposable gloves I extract one. I pull it around my right hand and flex my fingers, feeling the stretch in the glove. Using the gloved hand I pick up the donut and squeeze it as hard as I can. Jam splats onto the paper bag underneath. I open my hand and let the compacted mess in the shape of the inside of my fist drop onto the paper bag, and look at it emotionlessly.

Disgusting.

Like those anti smoking ads where they put out a cigarette in a fried egg. Nobody would desire such a thing. Not even I. There: once more I have conquered the evolutionary desire to eat. I take off the glove and crush it together with the destroyed donut inside the paper bag and bin the whole thing in the wastepaper basket.

Then I take out a notebook from the drawer. Carefully I tear a page. I tear a small piece from that page and put it into my mouth. I chew carefully and slowly before I swallow the fairly tasteless mush. I eat five pages before the hunger pangs die away. I close the book and put it away.

Feeling virtuous I go to the weighing machine and stand on it. I take a deep breath and look down.

Idling under eight stone.

Good.

I shift my weight around and the needle remains constant.

Very good.

I have to be extra careful with my intake of calories today because tomorrow I am having lunch with Lana and Billie. I look to the windowsill where I have stood Lana's wedding invitation with its bespoke caviar design across the inside of the envelope.

Then I turn towards the wall opposite my bed.

It is entirely covered with photos of Jack Irish. Some I have blown up.

Oh yeah! That's the other reason why I hate Lana Bloom. On my thirteenth birthday with the whole of my newly thirteen-year-old heart I fell deeply and irrevocably in love with Jack. And deeply in love with him I remain to this day.

Unfortunately, he is under the mistaken impression that he is besotted with her.

Two

I wake up early the next morning. There is no fogginess to clear away. Immediately it hits me. Today I am not going to work but am having lunch with Lana and Billie, and afterwards, we are going for Lana's fourth and most probably final fitting for her wedding gown. Billie and I will also be trying on our bridesmaid's dresses for the first time. I leap out of bed. There is so much to do. I strap on my sports bra, pull on a pair of black leggings and tie my hair into a ponytail high on my head.

Quick glance at the bedside clock. Nearly 7.00 a.m.

I spread a yoga mat on the carpet and a towel on top. Sitting on it I begin with some warm-up moves—slow, deep stretches. Then I lie down and do double my usual quota of stomach exercises, making sure that with every sit-up I punish my muscles mercilessly. I bound upwards energetically, take a sip of water from a plastic water bottle, and, alert to my rapidly increasing heartbeat, skip five hundred times on the spot. I come to a stop and, panting hard, wait thirty seconds. Then I continue skipping as fast as I can for another thirty seconds. I do the start and stop thing seven times.

By now I am drenched in sweat, my muscles are screaming and I am exhausted. I stick my headphones on and with music blaring into my ears I give over to twenty minutes of non-stop aerobics. I take off the headphones and slow down with thirty minutes of Callanetics. I do a hundred repetitions of each of the deliberately micro-small sets of movement. Every tiny contraction causes me burning pain, but it does not deter me until the entire routine is complete. I stand up and wipe the sweat dripping off me with an old towel.

I feel alive, strong and... prepared.

Taking a bucket full of cleaning solutions I leave my room—locking my bedroom door even though everyone is still asleep—and go into the bathroom. For about fifteen minutes as I do every day, I bleach and clean the sink, toilet bowl, shower cubicle, the tiles on the walls and the floor until they sparkle. Flushed and hot I step into the shower and turn on the tap. The shock of the ice-cold water hitting my head and shoulders makes me gasp. Just before my teeth start to chatter I twist the hot water tap and allow the water to become warm. The pleasure is indescribable.

Soaped and shampooed I step out and dry myself with a clean towel. Wrapping the damp one around my body and another around my head

I make my way back to my room. It is almost eight thirty by now. No one else is awake and the flat is still and quiet. If I put my ear to any of the other bedroom doors I will hear slow, heavy snores.

I sit in front of the mirror and gently massage my toweled head. Scrubbing hard damages the hair shaft. When I pull away the towel my hair is a wavy blue-black mess in the mirror. I part my hair and peer at the roots to see if my true color, a soft brown that turns the color of golden syrup and wheat in summer, is showing, but it is not. For many years I chemically straightened my hair, but a few months ago my hair began falling out, so now I am down to hot plates every time I wash my hair.

I plug the hair straightener into the socket, the light comes on, and I set about applying a ten-pence-sized squirt of protective cream on the palm of my hand and working it into my hair. With the blow dryer set on medium heat I begin to dry my hair. I work carefully because it is only last night that I glued on my acrylic nails and I don't want them ruined. They are long and pink and look good against my black hair. I adore them but can't have them all the time; I work as a florist.

When my hair is dry I gather thin lots between my fingers and pass them through the heated plates. Twenty minutes later my hair is a shiny black curtain falling six inches below my shoulders. I apply some wax to the ends and turn my head from side to side the way they do in shampoo adverts. The curtain swings just like it does in the ads.

Pushing my eyelids open one at a time, I slip in my colored contact lenses. I blink quickly a few times. They settle in. I look at myself in the mirror. My dishwater color irises are now blue.

Blue eyes and black hair—just like Lana.

I lean forward and unscrew the cap of the foundation bottle. I apply a fine layer with a damp sponge, carefully working towards my ears and blending into my hairline. That done, I pat compact powder onto the base. I pick up a magnifying mirror and check that the job is flawless. It is.

Time for color. First the eyes. Resting my right elbow on the dressing table top to steady it, I slowly pull the eyeliner brush around my eyes minimizing the slight upwards slant. I do the same to the other eye. Already my eyes look as big and as straight as Lana's.

Time to open them up: four layers of mascara. Using a combination of eye pencil and mascara and light feathery strokes, I color my eyebrows to match my hair. I tinge the apples of my cheeks with pink. Now for the hard part. I use a lip pencil and expertly draw my lips thicker than they are. The line is faultlessly even. I paint inside it. I wish I could afford those collagen injections that celebrities are always having done. But I can't so this will have to do.

I lean back slightly and look at myself and feel happy with the heavily painted mask the world will see. I dress in a white lace top, a cropped pink and white candy striped jacket and a darker pink mini skirt.

I fasten a sparkly, three-row necklace of glass beads set in zinc and linked together like chainmail around my neck. If I had seen it in a store's display case I would never have bought it, and to be perfectly honest, I don't think it looks all that, but the Duchess of Cambridge wore one at the royal screening of *Mandela: Long Walk To Freedom* and all the papers and magazines called it a drool-worthy, stunning style statement. So I rushed to Zara and queued up to buy it. Just in time to snatch the second last one. It had only cost £19.99. What's good for a Duchess...

Sourly, I wonder what Lana will wear now that she has all that money. She'll probably come dripping in diamonds. I step into a pair of white court shoes with soft pink polka dots. They are difficult to manage. They are not tight, simply badly designed. But they were cheap and look like a pair I have seen Paris Hilton wearing. Slowly and deliberately, so as not to stumble, I walk towards the mirror. I look at my reflection and a flutter of nervous self-doubt begins in my belly.

I quell it—you're not fat anymore.

I pick up a bottle of perfume and spraying it into the air on top of my head walk through the fine mist. I do this three times. For good measure I stop breathing and, facing the spray nozzle at my body, spray it all around myself.

I put my credit card and mobile phone into a small white Louis Vuitton handbag (fake, obviously) and stand before the mirror. My eyes are curiously blank. I gaze at my waist. Wasp tiny.

Not bad.

I turn back and look over my shoulder at the reflection of my derrière. That's French for butt, by the way. I found that out in *Marie Claire*. The material is snug on my hard won, tantalizingly small rear.

Not bad at all.

Three

Glamour (*'glaeme*) American **Glamor** noun

1. An air of magic or enchantment—specifically, a deceptive, bewitching and dangerous beauty or charm. Linked to spells of sorcerers, glamour indicates a mysterious, exciting magnetism dependent on artifice and falsification—make-up, beautiful clothes etc.
2. *Archaic* A magic spell; enchantment, specifically to bewitch and glorify by deceptive illusion causing a kind of haze to fall over the beholder, so things are seen in a form different from reality in order to possess or control the beholder to manipulate others into forbidden or dangerous actions.

I can afford a taxi since I won't have to pay for lunch so I call a minicab. The driver is a Cockney lad who glances into the mirror and tells me I look like a flower arrangement. 'You even smell like one,' he says.

I keep my voice cool. 'Thank you.'

'I love a girl who takes the time to dress up. Nowadays it's hard to tell women from men. What with everyone wearing the T-shirts and jeans uniform.'

I make the mistake of looking into his rear-view mirror. He is watching me. I smile distantly.

'Maybe we can meet up and go out for a drink sometime?'

As if I would go out with a taxi driver. I hate swearing, but it is precisely idiots like these that get me going. Fucking imbecilic moron.

'Thanks, but I've got a boyfriend,' I say frostily.

'Can't blame a bloke for trying...' He shakes his head regretfully, as if he ever stood any chance of going out with me.

I turn my head towards the moving scenery and for the rest of the journey keep my eyes firmly and deliberately away from him while I fume silently. Lana gets the billionaire and I get minicab drivers coming on to me. When we reach my destination he leers at me as he fumbles around for change from my tenner.

'Here you are, love.'

I hold my hand out. I don't tip him.

He drives off and I look up at the building. Pretty impressive. The lobby is clean, but unremarkable. I take the lift, walk along a beige corridor lit with wall sconces, and stop outside apartment fourteen. I ring the bell. Sash's *Ecuador* is blaring inside. I wait a few minutes but no one comes to open the door. I take my mobile out and tap into it.

'I'm outside.'

Billie opens the door in her bra and knickers. 'Be a few minutes more,' she shouts over the music. 'Make yourself at home. Help yourself to anything you find in the fridge and look around, but if you get bored come into my bedroom.' Leaving the door open she disappears down a corridor while I stand in the living room looking around me.

Oh! Wow.

I have been to Billie's room when she was living with her mum and it was done up in many colors and fun, but always a bit messy. But this, this is grown-up and seductively elegant. Like one of those sophisticated Parisian flats. With palm trees in bronze pots, a fainting couch and a low divan that has a peacock with a spread tail embroidered on it. There are scatter cushions in bright pink, a crystal pig on the coffee table and tapestries on the walls.

One wall is papered with richly colored birds on winding vines on a deep blue background. The curtains are all floor-length and expensively heavy with green, blue and pink tassels as thick as fingers. The nooks and crannies hold bronze and lapis lazuli lamps. At night they must create a soft amber glow for Billie.

A large, elegant armchair signals the end of the living room. Behind it thick drapes section off an intimate dining room with a green marble topped table and ruby chairs. I stand for a moment absorbing the foreignness of it all—the mirror, the beautiful intricately carved silver fruit bowl filled with fruit—and cannot help the envy that pours into my heart.

Not only Lana but even Billie is now living like a queen.

If I get close to Lana will her billionaire fiancé get me a flat like this too? And a fruit bowl that will always be full?

I walk towards the French door into the balcony. There are bamboo plants in blue pots and a stone water feature. The gurgling, splashing sound it makes is soothing. I look down at the scenery, the canal, the pretty houses, restaurants and bars with surprise. What a difference a cab ride can make. It almost feels as though I am in a different country. No trace of the concrete jungle here!

I grip the metal rail and feel sad.

Then I steel myself, turn away and walk through the corridor along the thick carpet. The first door I open is a baby's room. It has a cot and lots of toys. I suppose Lana's son must spend nights here. I close that door and open the next. A second bedroom. There is a desk untidy with piles of sketches. I go towards the desk and look at some of them. Billie did say I could look around. Baby clothes as colorful as parrots adorn the pages. I am surprised by how lovely they are. But what is Billie doing designing baby clothes?

The music has either come to an end or Billie has switched it off. I close the door softly and pass a bathroom—the wall and ceiling are cloudy gray marble. The most surprising thing about her bathroom is the polished mahogany toilet seat. Thick and broad, I imagine it must be an antique. A few more steps brings me to the threshold of a stunningly impeccable kitchen. Even the grouting between the floor tiles is pale and clean. Either Billie never cooks or she is a cleaning beast. Knowing Billie as I do, I'll stick with the first option.

There is a tin of baby biscuits on the otherwise barren kitchen table. The sink is empty and dry. All the granite surfaces are as clean as two new pins. I open the fridge. It keeps a pizza box of leftovers, some bars of chocolate and a carton of orange juice. There is a bottle of vodka and a tray of ice cubes in the freezer. I close it and go back to Billie's bedroom. The room stinks of hairspray.

Billie puts the can down and turns towards me. Her hair is the color of teal. It kind of suits her.

'Didn't you get yourself a drink? I've got vodka.'

I shake my head. 'I'm all right.'

It's bad enough that we will be having Chinese food. That stuff is loaded with MSG. And MSG is the stuff researchers feed rats to make them fat fast. My eyes run over Billie's body. She has the type of body that Pink the singer has. Firm and muscular. I guess Billie carries it off well, but in my books that's just one step away from running into fat. I am surprised to see that her legs are unshaved. She catches me staring in the mirror.

'Don't worry, I'll shave before I get into that bridesmaid dress,' she says, amused by my blatant curiosity.

'I...' Oh good God, she probably thinks I'm lusting after her.

Billie laughs at my expression. 'Sorry, but I don't sleep with straight girls.'

Suddenly all the years of working to better myself drop off a cliff. Deep down inside me I know nothing has changed. I am still the fat unattractive kid with the hairstyle that looks like a mental illness. Chased and bullied and monstrously ugly. Blood slams into my head. For a lightning moment I imagine rushing at her, my nails curved like talons. They pierce the jelly of her eyes.

Then she winks at me and I realize it was just a joke to cover an uncomfortable moment. She didn't mean any harm. It was me who had been rudely staring at her unclothed body. With that knowledge all is forgiven. She is the kid I always wanted to befriend, the coolest girl in school. The other kids were merciless, but neither Lana nor she ever took part in shaming me.

I smile back. 'You've done up the place real nice.'

'It's easy to make something look good when you have no budget constraints.'

'Really?' My voice is incredulous. 'You were allowed to have anything you wanted?'

Billie nods and puts away the hairdryer.

 24

'What's Blake like?' I ask curiously. I have only met Lana's man once at a party when he came to collect her. Intimidating as hell. As if chiseled from stone he stood in our midst, haughty, disdainful, and broadcasting universal sex appeal. Suddenly our eyes met across the room. His had poured over me like iced water, found nothing of interest and dismissively moved on. It was clear that he found us *all* utterly beneath him. He had not stayed long.

'Banker boy?' Billie says. There is indulgence and genuine affection in her voice. 'He can be cold-blooded, but he's always been good to me and he loves Lana.' She pauses. 'In fact, don't think I've ever seen a man so passionately in love. He loves her more than anything or anyone else in this world.'

A shaft of white-hot jealousy stabs me in the gut. Lana gets it right every time. Not only has she snared a billionaire, but one who is completely smitten with her. I make a huge effort to keep my smile in place.

'What about his son?'

'He would give up his life for the boy, but if Sorab and Lana were drowning, and he could only save one, there would be no hesitation. No matter what it cost him it would always be Lana.'

I lapse into silence and wonder what it must be like to be so treasured. No one has ever loved me, let alone so desperately. Billie slides open a cupboard and takes out a purple T-shirt that screams I MIGHT SAY YES in green and a pair of banana yellow jeans. She dresses quickly, pulls on a pair of leopard print boots with red soles and, snagging a man's black leather jacket from a hanger, turns towards me.

'Shall we go?'

We hail a cab and it drops us off outside the restaurant. This is where Billie and Lana often meet for dim sum. Lana has telephoned to say she is running late. We go in without her. The restaurant has no natural light. The walls are lacquered black, the carpet under our feet is the color of soot and the place is lit only with strategically placed spotlights that make the tablecloths rise out of the dark ground like very white lilies in a pond. We take our seats. I choose one that faces the door. I want to watch Lana come in.

A waitress comes to hand us our menus and ask what we would like to drink.

'Vodka,' pips Billie.

'Chinese tea,' I say more slowly.

I have just taken my first sip when Lana comes in carrying her baby. Every head in the room turns to look. A knife twists in my heart.

She is the living embodiment of that elusive quality: glamour.

Four

He has a silly name, Sorab. I would have called him Brad. He looks like a Brad, with sparkly blue eyes fringed by long curling lashes and the most solemn face you ever saw in a child.

'So sorry I'm late,' Lana apologizes breathlessly, and going around the table kisses first Billie and then me on the cheek. Her skin is softly perfumed and her lips are soft as they rest briefly on my skin. Strangely, the kiss from my sworn enemy doesn't cause me to flinch inwardly. In fact, some part of me welcomes the feel of it.

Both Billie and I assure her that she is not late, we have only just arrived ourselves. While she settles Sorab into a high chair and ties some highly colored toys to it and Billie is fussing over the child, I surreptitiously watch her over my menu. In truth I am shocked.

I had expected designer gear, Manolo Blahniks and diamonds, but she is dressed simply in a beige cashmere jumper that comes to her hips, black drainpipe jeans and a pair of those unfussy, flat-heeled riding boots you see in equestrian magazines. They look like nothing but cost the earth.

'Are you guys ready to order?' she asks, opening her menu, and the massive rock in her engagement ring blinds me.

'Goodness!' I exclaim. 'How many carats is that?'

Lana looks embarrassed. 'Ten.'

'Wow! Can I see it?'

She holds her hand out to me and I take it. Her fingers are finely boned and elegant, the skin soft and unblemished. I feel ashamed of mine. My stubby digits are scratched by rose thorns, and the knuckles scarred and grazed from forcing my fingers down my throat to induce vomiting. Suddenly even my beautiful pink nails look garish and brazen.

Under the spotlights of the restaurant the stone—an oval cut pink diamond—is so dazzling it is almost impossible to look away from its brilliance. To show off the vividly pink flawless stone it has been mounted on a plain band without any fuss or embellishments. I recognize the design. I have seen it before.

'It's a Repossi, isn't it?'

Lana looks surprised and impressed. 'Yes. How did you know?'

'I saw it in a magazine.'

'How observant you are, Jules? It is custom, but the setting is from a collection called Tell Me Yes.

'It's very, very beautiful.'

'Thank you.'

I release her hand, the ancient envy stirring, stretching, in a foul mood.

The waitress comes around and Lana orders green tea. Immediately, I wish I had ordered that. It sounds far more exclusive than plain old Chinese tea. I make a note to order that in future.

We order a selection of dishes and the menus are taken away.

'I thought your wedding card was really nice.'

Lana smiles. 'Good. I'm glad you like it. I wanted Sorab to be included.'

'Personally, I think you should have done a badass zombie invite. Not even death will do us part sort of thing,' Billie says.

'You can do that when you get married,' Lana retorts.

'I'm never getting married. I need the government to charge me to say I do like I need a fucking hole in the head.'

'Really? You *never* want to get married?' I ask.

'If I do marry it'll be barefoot on a beach with not a single official 'vested' with the authority to marry people in sight. No wedding dress, no cake, no guests. Just the sun, the sea, the sand, the coconut trees and an obliging bartender.'

Lana laughs.

'So how are the wedding plans coming along?' I ask.

'Well, to be perfectly honest, I have no idea. Blake has forbidden me to do anything. He says it's only six hours of our life, and no way is he going to let me ruin four months of our life getting stressed out with preparations. So, I have been confined to choosing the venue, contributing to the guest list, and everything to do with my dress.'

She beams at us, totally unaware of my animosity towards her.

'Ah, so it was you who picked a small church in Woburn and the reception at Wardown Towers.'

'Yes.' She smiles softly.

'Why? Why not somewhere glamorous like the Savoy or the Ritz?'

Lana touches her son's cheek and smiles at him before turning to me. 'Wardown Towers is an amazing place. It is surrounded by a hundred and ninety acre park teaming with deer, forests, lakes and meadows.' She stops and looks again at Sorab. 'But the real reason is that I wanted Blake's sister to be not only present but comfortable. She is in her twenties, but she has the mental age of a child. Since Wardown is where she lives it seemed the perfect location. Besides, I always dreamed of a reception in a beautiful spring garden.'

I wonder about this spastic sister that my search on the Internet did not uncover. Who is she? And why is Lana bending backwards to accommodate her? But all I say is. 'That's nice of you.'

On the other side of the table Billie is waving to a waitress. I know what she wants. The waitress comes and Billie points to her empty glass.

'So,' I say casually. 'Who do we know that are coming for the wedding?'

'Well, a few of our school friends, Amanda, Nina, Sylvia, Jodie—'

'No, what I meant is who is coming from our neighborhood?'

'Oh! Uh... Mary—'

'Fat Mary?' interjects Billie.

'Yes.'

'You invited Fat Mary?' Billie repeats, shocked.

'Yeah, I did.'

'Why?' both Billie and I ask in unison.

Lana takes a sip of tea and looks at Billie. 'Sometimes on my way to visit you, I'd take the way past the flats where we used to live so I could look at our old homes. That one time Mary was coming up the street. I crossed the road to avoid her, but she then crossed the road to join me. She took my hand and said she'd heard that mother had died. "Sorrow is how we learn to love," she told me.

'I was shocked. Is this really the woman who tanks up on a bottle of Cava, squeezes into a Lycra dress every Saturday night and goes up the road to look for a stranger to have sex with? "I know what you're thinking, but it is just something to do in this sad world," she said. I realized that I had misjudged her. She was so much more. We became friends.'

I look at Lana and suppress the annoyance I feel. This conversation has gone askew. 'So Fat Mary is coming. Who else from our neighborhood?'

'Oh my God!' Billie cries suddenly. She looks totally revolted.

'What?' Lana asks.

'Is that woman eating a chicken foot?'

Lana and I turn in the direction of her gaze. Indeed something resembling a dark brown chicken foot with the claws still attached is dangling from the woman's chopsticks. Sickened, I watch her delicately nibble at one end. What can be in a chicken foot? Skin, gristle, and in the pads—*fat*. Uh! yuck. The thought turns my stomach and I turn away.

'For God's sake don't stare,' Lana whispers.

'I'd rather starve than eat one of those,' Billie declares.

'It's meant to be a delicacy,' Lana informs.

I feel like screaming with frustration. Once again the conversation is drifting away from what I want to talk about. I realize I have no choice but to reveal my hand. 'What about Jack? Is he coming?' I ask as casually as I can.

Both Lana and Billie look at each other.

'Jack has been invited, but I don't know if he will come.'

That look they exchanged. There is more to this and I know exactly what to do to find out. When at an impasse, leave.

'I need to go to the toilet. Be back soon,' I say, and smoothly slide off the chair. I make it around the wall, behind where our table is, and drop my purse. Then I crouch down and pretend to be picking up stuff that has rolled to the floor while I hear every word of their conversation.

'Has he not been in touch then?' Billie asks.

'No. I really hoped he would come.'

'He's hurting, babe.'

'I guess I always thought he would give me away at my wedding.'

'It doesn't matter if he doesn't. You're marrying the man of your dreams.'

'I know, I know. I don't want to be selfish, but I love him so much and I really thought he'd be there, forever. To be honest I even find it hard to imagine getting married without him. And... He promised he'd give me away.' Her voice breaks, and she says something else, but I am interrupted by a stupid woman who has squatted down beside me.

'Here, let me help you,' the do-gooder says cheerfully, picking up my mobile phone and lipstick. I could have hit her. Because of her meddling I didn't hear the rest of Lana's words or Billie's reply. I snatch my phone and lipstick out of her hand and she shakes her head, surprised and disgusted by my rude behavior.

She stands up in a huff. 'Whatever,' she says, and marches away.

Two more women talking loudly in Chinese come towards me, and I have no choice but to stuff my things into my bag and stand. Irritated that I missed the most important part of the conversation, I head in the direction of the Ladies. I stand in front of the mirror and look at my reflection for a minute, my brain working frantically. Have Lana and Jack fallen out? My heart bursts with joy at the thought. I check my teeth for lipstick and then I go back to the table.

Both of them turn smiling faces towards me.

'We were just reminiscing about the past. About that time Billie didn't want to do PE and she told her teacher that she didn't want to change into her shorts because her legs were full of bruises where her mother had beat her.'

'How was I to know that Social Services would turn up at my door that evening?'

'Her mother made her take her trousers off and show the two women her legs.'

Billie makes a face. 'They should have seen the backs of my legs after they left! Crimson and purple.'

'We could hear the slaps and wallops from our flat,' Lana adds, laughing gleefully with the memory.

I titter politely to show interest.

'At least I wasn't a vain crybaby like you.' Billie looks at me. 'Once she took a pair of scissors to her own hair, made a total mess, and her mother had to cut what was left real close to her head. That afternoon she goes to buy an ice cream and the ice cream van guy says to her, "Here you go, sonny." What does madam do? She throws the ice cream on the ground in a hissy fit and runs home bawling, "He thought I was a boy."'

'I was only six then,' Lana defends, and then... They both look at me. Obviously wanting me to share the highlights of my childhood with them. I blink. My stories. Oh no! Under no circumstances am I returning to my friendless state or the horror that my despicable fat self endured. I cover the fact that my lips are quivering by taking a drink. A question pops into my head.

'You were in Iran for a year. What was it like?'

That sobers Lana up plenty.

'Iran is very beautiful, but when I first went there I was very sad. At that time it felt like my life was ruined. I was crazy about a man I could never have and I was pregnant with his child. I hardly went out and I never mixed with our neighbors. I couldn't speak Farsi anyway, so there was no real interaction, but they were always smiling at me, always nice—'

'Nice! Aren't they mostly terrorists?'

Lana's eyes flash. 'When you read the papers and listen to the news have a care. You are listening to that particular piece of news above all else that is happening in the world because somebody wants you to hear that. Have you ever wondered, Julie why we need to hear that Justin Bieber has been arrested for some minor infringement twenty times a day? Did nothing else important happen that day?'

I frown. Justin Bieber being arrested is important news—well, I want to know about it, anyway. And they repeat the news so that all his millions of fans get to hear about it. I glance quickly at Billie, but she is nodding in agreement. Seems I am the odd one out.

'After my mother died,' Lana continues, 'I saw my neighbors, the ordinary Iranians, for what they really are. I thought I was sad before, but when she was suddenly taken away from me I became lost. I couldn't do anything. I sat staring at a wall all day.

'I know you won't understand, but over the years our roles had changed. I was no longer the child, but the caregiver, the mother. I cried for her as a mother cries for her child. I could not bear to see her broken body, but neighbors, they were amazing. Though it was not their way—they are Muslims—they cleaned off the red polish on her toenails and painted them pale pink, powdered her face, colored her lips with her favorite lipstick, and placed her favorite rosary in her hand.'

The memory must still be very painful, because Lana's eyes glisten with tears. She bends her head and stares at the tablecloth.

'They shined my shoes for me, Julie! And the men, they arranged everything. The coffin—it had a brass nameplate and a satin and lace interior, the funeral in a sunny chapel, the Christian cemetery plot across town. Everything was done properly, with the greatest respect. They even laid one of Sorab's toys inside the coffin.'

She shakes her head in admiration for the people that I had been persuaded to believe should have glass and sand pancakes for breakfast.

'In the days after the funeral the women brought food three times a day, they took care of

Sorab, they found a nurse to breast-feed him because my milk had dried up, they cleaned the house, they shopped, they cooked. They are the kindest, most beautiful people I have ever met and if ever you have the chance, you must go there and decide for you for yourself if they are terrorists or they are simply like you and me.'

The food arrives. There is too much, but nobody else seems to think so. Billie and Lana both know how to eat with chopsticks. I ask for a fork and spoon. I watch Billie dip her dim sum into soy sauce and put it whole into her mouth. I pick up a shiny white dumpling. Under its transparent skin I can see...stuff, well pork, prawns and crab to be precise, and I put it into my bowl. I am so hungry my mouth is running with saliva, but I cut a tiny piece and slip it between my lips. It is so delicious my eyes actually widen.

'Good, isn't it?' Lana asks.

I nod and cut another tiny piece.

I chew slowly and watch Lana reach for the small plastic container and spoon she had taken out of her bag earlier.

'Shall we have some lunch?' she says, in that high sing-song voice that people put on when they are talking to babies and animals and ties a bib around her baby's neck. He smiles up at her and she begins to spoon food into his face. 'If you finish all your food you can have some of Auntie Billie's fried ice cream.'

The rest of the lunch is a stressful, exhausting ordeal with me pretending to eat the same amount as them. Believe me, it is a feat considering the little baskets of dim sum arrive with exactly three pieces in them. Two I palm and they end up inside my handbag. Despite all their attempts to include and pull me into the conversation I feel excluded and jealous of their obviously tight bond. When the fried ice cream arrives I sigh with relief. From my seat I smell it, though. Freshly fried batter and vanilla. A tantalizing combination that makes me twitch in my seat. The baby gets some too. He seems to love it. As soon as it is all gone, Billie stands up.

'I'm off to suck a fag,' she says, picking up her box of cigarettes.

I kind of panic at the thought of being left alone with Lana. 'Smoking will give you cancer.'

'Great, that'll save me from dying of boredom,' she quips and then she is gone.

I look at Lana and she is pulling a wet-wipe out of its box and cleaning her baby's hands. Terrified that an uncomfortable silence will descend upon us I blurt out the first thing that comes into my mind.

'How old is he now?' As if I'm interested.

'Fourteen months tomorrow.'

'He's a very quiet baby, isn't he?'

'Yes, he is like his father. Blake's first language is silence.' She glances at me with a smile. 'When he was young his capacity for silence was such that his parents thought there was something wrong with him.'

'Do you think you will have more kids?'

Lana glows. 'For sure. At least two, but most probably three.'

'Oh.' Does she not care that having so many kids will ruin her body? I suppose now she has the money she can go and remodel her body in any way she wants.

'There you go. All done,' she tells her son and turning to me says, 'He hates it when any part of him gets dirty.' She puts the soiled wipe on the table. 'I got a little gift for you to say thank you for being my bridesmaid, but I was in such a rush this morning, thanks to him,' she rolls her eyes in the direction of the child, 'I forgot to bring it. If you don't have anything planned for this evening perhaps you'd like to come home with me after the fitting? We can have tea together.'

I can barely believe it. I am dying to see where Lana lives now. I school my voice so I don't sound too eager. 'That would be nice, thanks.'

Lana pays the bill and we are thankfully out of the restaurant. I take a deep breath of the cool air. That is the last time I go to a restaurant with them.

The Bentley arrives and we all climb into it. Inside it is the byword in comfort. I settle in and we are borne towards that girlie ceremony called a dress fitting.

Five

I am the thief of secrets. For I have learned the ritual of being quiet. I can become so still, it is as if I become invisible, and people forget I am there and begin to take me into their labyrinth of secrets.

—Julie Sugar

Lana disappears behind the curtain with a seamstress called Rosie and her assistant, whose name I didn't catch. Strange, but I must admit I feel a surge of excitement. What is it about wedding dresses? Most of them are like meringues and yet... Perhaps it is the idea of a bride. I try to imagine what Lana's dress might be like. Obviously floor length. But I have never seen a custom-made dress that has been flown across half the world twice and requires four fittings. As Lana explained in the car the first fitting was for when the dress was skeletal, the second when it was half complete, the third when it was almost compete, and this fourth and last fitting when it needs only to be zipped up.

Five minutes pass.

Sorab has fallen asleep in his pushchair and Billie is lounging on one of the long sofas playing with her phone. I walk around the large space. It belongs to some other designer, but Lana's designers, two Australian men, have rented it for the afternoon. The late afternoon sun is low in the sky and soft silver light is filtering through. I go to the window and look at the street below.

I have only the view of the back of another gray building, but I love London. Every time I come to London I start to feel alive. On the street below two men are standing by a lamp post casually looking around them. I recognize them. They were at the restaurant too. From behind me comes the soft rustle of Billie's trouser legs brushing against each other as she crosses and uncrosses her legs.

I turn back and glance at her. She is still messing about with her phone. I leave the window and go to the long table pushed up against one end of the room and glance at the stuff on it. Dressmaker's chalk, sketches, fabric samples, a curved ruler, a pair of scissors, a length of lace.

And I think of the two men outside.

'Out she comes,' Rosie calls in her strong Australian accent and starts pulling the curtain aside.

Billie springs up and comically starts singing, 'Here comes the bride.' But she stops mid-sentence, gasping, her hands flying to her cheeks when all of Lana, head dipped to avoid the hanging material, comes out from behind the curtain. Even my mouth falls open. The dress is breathtakingly exquisite—couture at its best—and Lana—Lana is unimaginably, *impossibly* beautiful.

I have literally never seen anything so lovely in my life.

Rosie describes the dress. I hear snatches. French lace, Italian silk, antique seed pearls, Swarovski crystals, mounted on Italian silk.

So let me describe it to you. It has a halter neck. The bodice is made from French lace that has been intricately embroidered and embellished with antique seed pearls and Swarovski crystals, and mounted onto Italian silk. The way the material molds to her body so seamlessly without even the tiniest puckering, sagging or bulging anywhere is truly amazing. Somewhere about the tops of her thighs it trumpets out into a ball gown—all tulle and layers and layers of organza, probably hundreds. The craftsmanship is astonishing. No wonder they needed four fittings.

'Oh, Lana, you look so beautiful,' cries Billie. Her voice sounds choked.

Lana grins happily and then looks to me.

'It's fantastic. You look...regal,' I enthuse, genuinely impressed and awed by the sight of Lana in her dress. And at that moment I don't feel like an outsider. We are joined in a beautiful ritual. Three friends who went to try out Lana's wedding dress. It connects us. I actually feel tears prickling the backs of my own eyes. No one has ever included me in their plans like this before.

'Turn,' commands Billie. Lana turns.

Now it is my turn to gasp. The dress is daringly cut right down to the small of her back, from where it unexpectedly takes a romantic turn and becomes the beginnings of a rose bustle. All the layers are petals of the most delicately conceived and dramatically executed rose I have ever encountered. The ends of some of the petals are frayed to give the impression of lustrous softness. The flowing layers finally sweep down to form the chapel train of the dress. The dress is risqué and perfect.

Jaws will hit the floor.

The two fitters lift the train off the floor and Lana goes to stand on the raised platform. 'There is a silver sixpence sewed into the netting of the dress,' Lana tells us.

Rosie beams with satisfaction. 'Doesn't she look gorgeous?'

'It's a show stopper, the best dress you will ever wear,' Billie declares.

'It's the most dazzling thing I've ever seen,' I say in agreement.

'Do you think the back is too low?' Lana asks, turning slightly to survey the long expanse of her naked back.

'Absolutely not,' I tell her firmly.

'It's going to give Blake one hell of a hard-on in the church,' Billie deadpans.

Lana breaks into an excited giggle, and it is so infectious that both Billie and I join in like giddy teenagers. She looks so happy. And for the first time in my life I don't begrudge her this happiness. Perhaps because I am part of it. This memory will remain bottled and fizzing in my mind.

We are still standing around in the warm glow of old friendships, when Rosie's assistant brings the bridesmaids' dresses out from a metal rack. Mine is a floor-length silk and organza number with a mermaid silhouette, sweetheart neckline and in the color I love most: the softest pink you could imagine. Rosie calls it blush. While Rosie and her assistant fuss and flap needlessly around Lana's totally perfect dress we try on our dresses and slip into shoes that have been fashioned from the same material as our dresses.

We come out from behind the curtain and Lana claps her hands with delight. I look into the mirror and have to agree. Both dresses are divinely beautiful with crystal scatters over the bodice and chest. The effect of the blush organza swirling around our silk clad feet is almost cloud-like. In the three-way mirror the layers of organza and Swarovski crystal unify our look and we complement Lana perfectly.

This is the first time I can compare what I look like beside Lana. I have always imagined that I am much bigger than her, especially during that time when she lost a lot of weight and was very much thinner, but it looks like we are both about the same size now. It is even possible that I might be, by a whisper, the thinner one. I am elated by my discovery.

'Are the two men outside bodyguards?' I ask.

'Yes,' Lana admits awkwardly. 'But they are mostly for Sorab.'

And yet a look passes between her and Billie.

There are secrets here. Smoothly I step backwards so I am no longer reflected in the mirrors. There is only Lana and Billie. I have become invisible.

'Has she tried to make contact again?' Billie asks.

'No, but last week I saw her across the road. She simply stood and stared at me.' Lana shudders with the memory.

'Did you tell Blake?'

'No. What could I say? She didn't do me any harm. And I don't think she will.'

'How many times do I have to tell you? Stop judging everybody by your standards. Just because you wouldn't do something doesn't mean someone else won't. She *is* going to try to harm you. You must tell Blake.'

'I don't know, Bill. He has a very high opinion of her. They've been friends since they were children, and he'll only think I am being petty and jealous.'

'Look, if you don't tell him I will.'

'All right, all right, I will.'

'Who is she?' I ask softly.

Both girls look at me. They had forgotten I was there.

'Victoria, Blake's ex,' says Lana guardedly.

'Blake's crazy ex. She's like Cleopatra and the serpent all rolled into one,' Billie supplies generously, but her voice is vicious.

Six

Billie kisses the sleeping child, Lana and then me, in that order, and slips into a black cab. The chauffeur helps put Sorab into the baby seat strapped in the front and Lana and I climb into the back of the car. The trip to her place is less uncomfortable than I thought it might be as Lana first gets a phone call from Blake. I know because her voice softens and a small smile curves her lips. I turn my head to look out of the window and pretend not to listen.

'Hi, darling. Yeah, we're done... Nope, no more fittings... It's absolutely beautiful... We're on our way home now. I forgot to bring Julie's present so I'm taking her back with me... Yeah... He's asleep... Good as gold. As usual.' He says something that makes her laugh. She is silent while she listens and then she giggles and says, 'Mmnnn...that sounds right up my street. Honestly can't wait.' She makes a kissing sound and ends the call.

I turn my head, a polite smile plastered on my face, and her phone rings again. 'Oh dear. Do you mind if I take this? It's the wedding organizer.'

'Not at all. Go ahead.'

Since her replies are mostly monosyllabic sounds of agreement I lose interest and stare out of the window. I wonder what her home will be like. By the time Lana ends her call we are already driving up to her apartment block. Not a whiff of low rent despair here. And, oh my, she lives right opposite a park too. We get out of the car and enter the building. It's all very posh and new-money flash inside. Lana waves to the Asian man sitting at the reception desk and he literally splits his face in two while executing an almighty grin.

We get into the lift, and in the confined space I find my first awkward moment. I turn quickly towards the baby. He is fast asleep in his pushchair. In sleep he looks angelic. I look up and Lana is looking at me.

'We're nearly there,' she says without the least trace of awkwardness.

I clear my throat, flash a smile, and turn to stare at the gleaming doors.

Lana drops her card key into a slot and we are standing in the kind of apartment I have only seen in magazines. I cannot help it. I draw a quick breath of surprise.

'I forget sometimes how beautiful it is,' Lana says, as she moves towards a long gray box that had been placed on a table near a large gilded mirror. I watch her in the mirror pull the red ribbons off it and lift the lid. I peek inside. My favorite. Long-stemmed yellow roses in a deep box. She reaches for the envelope inside and pulling out the card reads, and smiles, a secret smile.

'From Blake?'

'Yes.' There is happiness in her voice. 'I'll give you a tour after I put him into bed.' She bends to pick the child up.

'Do you need help?'

She lifts the sleeping child in her arms. 'No, I can manage. I am actually dreading the day I will no longer be able to carry him.'

Silently, I follow her into the boy's bedroom. The trompe l'oeil on the walls gives the illusion we are floating in a blue sky filled with fluffy white clouds. There is a white cot, a playpen and enough toys to fill a toyshop in the room. I stand back and watch her gently place the boy in the cot, take his shoes off, and smooth the hair away from his forehead. She turns to me.

'Want that tour now?'

I nod.

So she takes me from room to room while I gawp and gape and struggle to still that snake of envy twisting and hissing in my heart. We used to be schoolmates. We used to live on a council estate. We were both grindingly poor. Yet, here she is living the perfect life. She has everything anyone could ever dream of having. She has made it and I have not.

'We won't be living here after the wedding. I'd like Sorab to have a garden to play in so we'll be moving to a house in Kensington Palace Gardens.'

Yeah right, billionaire's row.

The thoughts die in my brain as Lana opens the master bedroom. Wow! Just wow! My eyes move to the bed. Three of my beds could fit into that massive thing. I have the irrational urge to go lie on the beautifully made luxurious sheets with its profusion of pillows.

'Come on,' Lana says. 'Your gift is in here.'

She opens a door and we are in a walk-in closet. She opens a cupboard and we are staring at a whole collection of to-die-for designer handbags. My dazed eyes fall on a Rene Lautrec bag. I have read about these bags in magazines and seen a picture of Madonna carrying one. Each one is handmade using the center cut from the belly of a grade-one, farm-raised American alligator, crocodile, stingray or South African ostrich. I never thought I would see one. As if in a trance I go to touch it.

'Blake gave that to me on Valentine's day.'

'It's beautiful,' I whisper, thinking of the rude card with pop up penis the van driver from the shop next door slipped through the letterbox of the florist shop where I worked.

'Yes, but I so hope you will think this is too...' She pulls out a box from the top shelf and holds it out to me.

I look at the box. It has Dior stamped on it. I am frozen. She bought me a Dior. A real Dior. I lift my eyes to her face. She is looking at me expectantly, a smile on her face.

'Go on,' she urges and moves it closer toward me.

I take the box, lift the lid, and take the bag out of its protective cover. If this is a dream I don't want to wake up. I hold it up. This year's collection. I have seen a photo of it being modeled on a Paris catwalk in last month's *Marie Claire*. I take my stupefied gaze away from the bag and fix it on Lana's face. She is looking at me with bright eyes and suddenly an image flashes into my mind.

I am twelve years old and running as fast as my fat body will allow me to. My brother's oversized oilskin coat is flapping behind me. I am panting, my breath is catching in my throat and my lungs burn as if on fire. Behind me are the shouts of boys. The yobs. The bullies. They are throwing stones at me.

'Yah, get her,' they shout.

One hits the back of my head and my foot catches on something on the ground. I pitch forward, the weight of my body pushing me through the air with frightening momentum. I land sprawled, face inches away from the ground.

I feel the tears stinging my eyes. I won't cry. I won't cry. I will stand up and face them. My knees are scraped raw and the palms of my hands are bleeding. Hyperventilating wildly, I roll over and sit up before I am surrounded by the jeering bullies. Desperately, I try to catch my breath. I can beat them. I wish then for a fierce dog, a pit bull that will grab their growing willies and bite them clean off. But I have no fierce dog. I reflect on my situation. The stones are only pebbles. It is not the stones, only the intent that hurts. I look up at them. I won't stand up to them today. I'll do whatever they want me to and they will let me go.

'It's a fat gorilla escaped from the zoo,' one of them says cruelly.

And then Lana is breaking through the circle like an avenging angel.

'Leave her alone,' she shouts, staring down boys that are twice her size.

'It's just a joke,' Jason, the leader of the gang, says.

'Look at her. She's bleeding,' Lana states angrily.

'She's so fat she tripped and fell on her own,' one of the boys says cheerfully, and they all laugh as if it is the funniest thing they have heard in years.

'Come on, guys,' Jason says, and they go away.

'Are you all right?' Lana asks, holding her hand out to me.

Ignoring her hand I heave myself up and without thanking her I run away. One day I will be thinner than you.

'If you don't like it, we can exchange it for something else,' says Lana from far away. She seems disappointed. She thinks I don't like her gift.

I smile suddenly, happily. 'No, I love it. I've never been given anything so beautiful in all my life.'

She flashes a relieved smile. 'Thank God. I think it's beautiful, but I wasn't sure if we have the same taste.'

We smile at each other.

'I was wondering if you would like to have a makeover. Have Bruce Lenhart restyle your hair? And let a really great make-up artist do your face?' For a split second her eyes slide down to my mouth. Then she is smiling again. Briefly I entertain the idea that my lipstick is smudged, but I know it is not. There is something wrong with my mouth. I become convinced it is an insult. She can keep her fucking makeover.

I start shaking my head. 'Please, Julie. It'll be fun. I looked so much better when they finished with me.'

But I like the way I look. I work very hard to maintain this 'look'.

'Even Billie has agreed.'

Bruce Lenhart? The idea is tempting. Celebrities go to him. It costs hundreds of pounds just for a simple haircut.

'But what if I go to him and he does something that I can't afford to keep up?'

'We'll tell him that he has to give you a style that can be maintained by you, hmnnn, what say you?'

Bruce Lenhart? Who was I kidding? Of course I want him to style my hair. 'All right.'

'Good.' She grins. 'Come on, let's go have some tea and we'll sort a date out for next week.'

We move into her kitchen. Vast. It reminds me of the yellow kitchen from that famous kitchen designer, I forget his name, that I keep seeing in all the mags. But unlike Billie's kitchen it is obvious that it is well used. I pop myself on a high stool facing the island while she fills the kettle with water. Her phone rings. She looks at it and appears surprised.

'Sorry, I have to take this,' she tells me and answers it. 'Brian... What?... No... That's OK... Let him come up.' She ends the call and slowly puts the phone on the counter. The kettle has boiled. The blue light has gone off.

'My father is downstairs,' she says. Her voice is soft, her eyes are pained. 'I won't be long with him, will you wait for me here in Sorab's room?'

'Of course,' I say, and slide off the stool.

'Are you all right?'

'Yes, yes, I'm fine.' She appears distracted. The phone rings again. She looks at it and picks it up eagerly.

'It's OK,' she says into the phone. 'No, please don't come, my darling. I'm fine... Really. It will be fine... I promise... I love you too...so, so much... I'll see you later tonight.'

The doorbell rings. She jumps. We look at each other. There is an odd expression of pain and longing in her eyes, which suddenly makes her seem a child again. I hate her. Why then do I want to hold her and comfort her? I take a step in her direction. She shakes her head and disappears in the direction of the front door. I stand for a minute in the kitchen, follow her down the corridor and enter Sorab's room. I stand at the door uncertainly. The boy is sleeping soundly. If I leave the door a quarter of an inch ajar I can see nothing, but I can hear everything.

'Hello, Dad.' Her voice is distant and strange. So different from what it has been all afternoon.

I don't recognize her father's voice. It has been so long. 'Look at you all grown up. You're so beautiful. Just like your mother.'

'Mum died last year.' Her voice is flat.

'I'm sorry to hear that, Lana.'

'Why are you here, Dad?'

'I read about your wedding in the paper.'

'Oh.'

'I believe I even have a grandson.'

'He's asleep.'

'We won't disturb him then.'

'Do you have other grandchildren?'

'Yes. Two.'

'That's nice. I suppose they get to see you all the time.'

There is a slight pause.

'Yes,' her father confesses softly. 'But I'm here now. Sorab—that's the little one's name, isn't it—will get to see his grandfather just as much.'

Lana says nothing.

'I'd like to give my daughter away at her wedding.'

'You can't. Billie's dad is giving me away.'

'That's a shame. That should be my privilege.'

'Dad, did you ever think what would happen to me if Mum had died after you left?'

He doesn't squirm, I'll give him that. Even though I cannot see his face the words that come out of him are smooth and well-oiled. 'If your mother had died then Social Services would have contacted me, and you would have come to live with me.'

'How would Social Services have contacted you, Dad? Did you leave a contact number with anyone?'

'Let bygones be bygones, Lana. I'm here now.'

'They would have taken me into care, Dad. Do you know what happens to kids in care? They get shunted around and abused! You simply didn't care either way, did you? You just went on and started a brand new family. Not once did you try to contact me. I am nothing to you.'

'I'm here now.'

'Why are you really here, Dad?'

'Look, I took care of you for years. That counts for something. We are blood.'

'How much, Dad?' Her voice is cold.

'I don't want your money.'

'Dad, you will never have a relationship with me. Your best bet is to name your price now or be forever silent.'

'All right. A hundred thousand.'

My eyes widen with shock, but Lana's answer is immediate. 'Done. I will have it transferred into your account by tomorrow.'

'Now that I think about it, you are rich beyond anything I can ever imagine. Can you make it two hundred thousand?'

Lana must have nodded because he thanks her.

'Goodbye, Dad.'

'I won't say goodbye to my own flesh and blood. You'll see me around, girl.'

I hear the door close and quickly come out. Lana is walking towards me. When we are about five feet apart she stops. Her shoulders are hunched, her face pale, but she is trying to be brave.

'What did he want?' I ask.

'What do you think?'

I say nothing.

'Come on, let's have some tea,' she says, but her mood is changed irreparably. She pours out the water that is already in the kettle into the sink and refills it. The kitchen is full of that noise. Suddenly she stops and puts the kettle down. Takes a deep breath.

'He never loved us,' she whispers. Her eyes are full of unshed tears. I was about to tell her to sit down while I make the tea when we hear the front door open. Before either of us can move Blake is standing in the kitchen doorway. For a moment they simply stare at each other.

'How did you get here so fast?' she gasps.

'I was closer than you thought,' he says simply.

With a great sob she rushes into his arms. I am invisible to either of them. He holds her in the tight circle of his arms.

'I'm so sorry, my darling. So sorry,' he whispers into the top of her head. She presses her cheek into his chest and squeezes her eyes shut. Forgotten by both of them I watch them with avid curiosity. So this is what the great man is like when he is with her. Tender. Gentle. As if she is irreplaceably precious. It makes me long for that sort of a love.

Lana lifts her head slowly and looks up into his face. There is something sad about the way he gazes into her eyes. It is as if it is he who has been wounded and not her. Billie is right, he truly, truly does love her. No yachts, no expensive toys, no helicopters. This was the real thing. They didn't need anything or anyone else. They were quite simply blissfully happy with each other.

'He came for money,' she says so softly I almost don't hear it.

'I know,' he soothes gently.

'I gave it to him.'

He raises his hand to her face, and with the back of his hand brushes her cheek. He does not ask how much Lana has given away, but says, 'You do know, he'll be back for more.'

'When I was very young he used to carry me on his shoulder. And he would make my mother laugh and laugh and laugh. In the end, does it matter that he didn't love me? Does that mean I should love him less?'

'Shall I arrange for him to receive an allowance?'

Lana nods. 'Yes, let him have his money. Let him be happy. I have you and Sorab. Why should I wish ill on anyone else? My mother forgave him. I didn't. I let it eat me up all these years. Let him be well.'

They don't hear it, but I do. The boy is awake in the other room. He is opening his door and making his way towards the kitchen. I make a small sound in my throat and Lana swivels her head in my direction.

'Oh my God, Julie. I'm sorry. I didn't invite you here to witness my family drama.'

But I am no longer looking at her. I am looking at Blake, how his eyes have frozen over as soon as they left Lana and found me in his kitchen. He flips out his phone from his pocket.

'Tom will give you a lift home,' he says and starts dialing. The speed at which Tom answers is impressive. 'Tom, can you pick Julie up from the lobby.'

The child, his face still sleepy, appears in the doorway.

Again I see a transformation in Blake's face. All the lines, all burdens in his shoulders leave. 'Lookie who's here,' he says, and, bending at the knee, opens his arms. The boy toddles over to him, little arms outstretched like a miniature Frankenstein. His small arms encircle his father's neck and his father kisses him and lifts him high into the air making him squeal with delight.

Lana turns towards me.

'I'll call you tomorrow and we'll arrange that makeover trip,' she says. I take my gift from the kitchen counter and we go out towards the front door. I feel strangely reluctant to leave. I want to stay and absorb the deep intimacy and happiness I have witnessed. I don't want to go back to my shitty home and my non-responsive, miserable family, all trapped in their layers of lard.

'Thank you for my present.' I smile, clutching the box.

Lana smiles back. She opens the front door and walks me to the lift. She presses the button to call it and it arrives very quickly. The door swooshes open.

'Call you tomorrow,' she says again, and the doors close on her.

Seven

The next time I see Lana is a week later, on a Thursday. She sends Tom to pick me up to bring me to her apartment. I sit inside the clean, softly scented interior of the Bentley wearing my best jeans, a top patterned with pink daisies teamed with a hot pink jacket and sandals with pink bows.

'I love your top,' she says as soon as she opens the door.

'Thank you,' I reply, but I am thrown into confusion. Does that mean she doesn't like the rest of my outfit? Lana is in a white sheath dress and a pair of deep red wedge shoes. White contrasts beautifully with her hair. She looks cool and understated.

There is a middle-aged woman in the apartment. Lana introduces her as Gerry, the nanny. She smiles pleasantly, and goes back into Sorab's room. She is taking the boy out to the park.

'Hello,' I greet the child.

He looks at me solemnly. There is a great deal of reserve about this child. He is eerily adult-like.

Lana is right, he is exactly like his father. The nanny leaves with the boy and Lana takes me into the kitchen.

'I baked a carrot cake yesterday. Want a piece?'

'That would be lovely,' I say, and climb onto the stool I had used the last time I was here. She already has a teapot ready. She puts a cup and saucer in front of me and pours some tea in. Then she pushes a sugar bowl and a jug of milk towards me.

'I like mine black,' I say with a smile, and bring the cup to my lip.

I watch her cut a slice of carrot cake and put it on a plate. It looks moist—crumbs fall onto the china. I look at the walnuts embedded in it and consider telling her that I have a nut allergy, and then I realize I want to try her cake. Perhaps it will be lousy. She comes around the island and places the cake in front of me. I break a tiny bit off and pass it into my mouth. It is freaking delicious. Sweet and oily. The way everything should be. Is there nothing that this woman will not do well?

'Well?' she asks, popping herself on the stool next to mine, a huge slice of cake on her plate. 'Do you like it?'

'Delicious,' I say, truthfully. She smiles at me warmly and I smile back.

I break off another small piece.

'You remind me,' she says, 'of those French actresses in the black and white movies that my mother used to watch. They used to break off minute pieces from their bread rolls or baguettes or whatever they were eating and slip them daintily into their mouths too.'

'Really? You used to watch black and white movies?' How boring. I break another piece.

'Sometimes. They were classy.'

We sit quietly for a minute, both sipping our tea.

'What do you do all day?' I ask.

'Well, Billie and I were planning to set up a baby clothes business.'

I nod. Ah, that would explain the colorful drawings I found in Billie's place.

'But,' she carries on, 'I realized that it would be a total waste of my time. The reason people take up jobs that they hate or start a business is to earn money. I have more money than I could possibly spend. I am in the process of starting a children's charity. I'll start in Britain but eventually it will be a worldwide organization. I'm calling it CHILD. I have to be careful, though. I don't want it to be like the other charities where so little actually gets to the intended recipients.'

She's right there. I just read that Lady Gaga's charity took in over two million and paid out one grant for five thousand dollars while hundreds of thousands were squandered on expenses.

She turns slightly away from me to look at the clock on the wall and I break a large piece of cake off and, with my hand under the counter, squeeze it into a ball in the palm of my left hand.

'Can I use your bathroom?'

'Of course. There is something wrong with the toilet in the cloakroom. Just use the one in my bedroom. Do you still remember where it is or do you need me to show you?'

'No, no, I remember.'

'OK,' she says, and forks another piece of cake into her mouth.

I go into her bathroom and flush the cake down the toilet, wash my hands quickly, and go back into her bedroom. Her laptop is open, but the screen has gone dark. I go to it and tap the mouse pad. The screen opens to an odd sight. It is a website about sex magick and secret cults! What the...? Huh?

I read the first paragraph of something titled The Emerald Tablets.

"Far in the past men there were who delved into darkness, and using

dark magick called up beings from the great deep below us. Forth came

they into this cycle, formless were they, existing unseen by the children

of earthmen. Only through blood could they become, only through

man could they live in the world."

Dark magick? Beings from the great deep below us? Formless ones? Blood rituals! What the hell is Lana doing on a crazy site like this? There is a notebook open by the laptop. I recognize Lana's handwriting. I scan through it.

El =Saturn
The worship of Saturn is the oldest secret religion.
Their symbol — the one eye
Why is the one eye symbol on the American dollar bill??
Symbols are perceived by humans on a subconscious level.
Is that why modern media and the entertainment industry is filled with one-eye symbols? Are celebrities flashing it without realizing its true meaning and what they are communicating to the public or are they puppets?
The occult symbols and imagery are everywhere, in movies, television, music and fashion, but human beings are totally blind to them.

The first and most important tenant of initiation into almost all cult sex magick is the sodomizing of children!!!! Sodomy and pedophilia is the foundation of the whole thing!! Goes back to Nimrod and the Egyptian initiations.
CANNOT proceed to the next level without this step.

Blake's dad!

Child sacrifice is a worldwide phenomenon. Every culture has at some point in history stooped to it. Why?
Is there a long-term agenda? An unseen hand?

Who are the children of the shadows? What do they want with us?
Need more answers. Can't find! Who to ask?

I can make no sense of her notes. Why is Lana doing research on sex magick and such dark subjects as child sacrifice? Why is Blake's dad

mentioned in the notes? And the sodomizing of children! Why is she interested in such an unspeakably horrible subject?

I run to the door and hurry down the corridor. In the kitchen Lana's slice of cake is almost gone and she is sipping her tea.

'Finish your cake,' she says. 'We should be going or we'll be late for our appointment.'

I sit down, my mind racing. I eat the rest of the cake without tasting it.

We have just got into the car when Blake calls. I can tell by the way her voice softens and becomes all giggly. I find it hard to marry up this love-struck girl/woman with the dark research I found on her laptop. If this is a mask she is wearing then it makes me determined to find out what is really going on. When she terminates the call I ask her if there will be paparazzi at the wedding.

'No, Blake has had the area designated as a no fly zone. It is just for close friends and family.'

'How come you're not having a bridal shower?'

'I guess because I don't want my friends to shower me with gifts. I already have *everything* I could possibly want!'

Wow! How amazing to be able to say that. 'What about a hen night? Don't you want one of those?'

'Blake doesn't want to have a stag night and even though he's cool with me having a night out with the girls I hate leaving him at night. I see so little of him as it is.'

'Why doesn't Blake want a stag night?'

'He says stag nights are a form of consolation for men who feel they are sacrificing a cherished state for the sake of love. He knows he is sacrificing nothing.'

'He works really hard, doesn't he?'

'Yes, very.'

'I thought rich people spent all their time quaffing champagne and caviar and going to the opera.'

'Blake's father didn't want his children to be trust fund kids. They were taught that even the greatest empire can be brought to its knees if the king and his favorites are sunk in luxuries and dissolution.'

Something flashed in Lana's eyes when she mentioned Blake's father. What, I do not know...yet.

Tom drops us outside Selfridges and Lana takes me to a make-up counter where an Asian girl smiles politely at me. Lana introduces us.

'Go on, work your magic,' Lana says. 'I'll be back in half an hour.'

First Aisha takes a photograph of me.

'Why are you doing that?'

'Usually women who are used to wearing very heavy make-up feel naked and dissatisfied when they first look in the mirror at what I have done, but they react in a totally different way to a Polaroid of themselves.'

I sit on a stool and she positions herself in front of me.

'Are you wearing colored contact lenses?'

I nod.

'Are they for correction purposes or just cosmetic?'

'Cosmetic.'

'Right.'

Going to a drawer she brings out antiseptic wipes and a contact lenses case and some storing solution. She gives the wipes to me and fills the cases with the solution and passes them to me. I clean my fingers and remove my lenses.

'You have such lovely hazel eyes,' she says. 'What a shame to cover them with those lenses.'

Then she wets a cotton wool pad with make-up remover and starts taking the layers off. Once it is all gone she takes a step back and looks at me carefully. 'Your eyebrows are so light. Is that the natural color of your hair?'

'Yes.' I grimace.

'Why do you do that? It's a beautiful color.'

She says no more. Just quietly gets to work. Lana comes back just as she is finishing. Her mouth becomes a surprised O and her eyes sparkle with delight.

'Oh, Julie,' she exclaims. 'You look stunning.'

Another photo is taken of me and then the stool is turned around. I look at the mirror.

And I am not pleased.

The girl looking back at me is too exposed. Too young. Too uncovered. Aisha brings the two photos and puts them into my hands. The photos tell a different story. One is harsh with black eyebrows, fake blue eyes and thickly painted lips and the other is a dewy and soft eyed. I know which one I prefer. I look in the mirror.

'I guess I am just not used to it,' I say uncertainly.

Lana comes close to me. 'Julie, you look beautiful. I have never seen you look more beautiful.'

'Really?'

'Really. Look, let's go do your hair, and then you can decide.'

Lana pays for my cosmetics and we leave. I catch a glimpse of myself in one of the mirrors and maybe, maybe Lana is right. I do look better. Different anyway.

Inside the fragrant air-conditioned confines of the hairdresser's, Bruce Lenhart's eyebrows fly into his hairline.

'What's the inspiration for this?' he asks, running his hands through my hair.

'Morticia Adams,' I say meekly. I'm not about to tell anybody that Lana is my inspiration.

He crosses his arms across his chest. 'Your hair is very dry. Do you straighten it as well?'

I nod.

'So your hair is curly.'

'Wavy.'

'And you have been coloring your hair for how long?'

'Years.'

'Let's get to work.'

As he works he explains that trying to bleach away years of chemicals is very harmful and he won't be able to strip it back to its natural color. But he will take away as much as he can, throw a medium brown dye on all of it, and add three shades of highlights everywhere, which will turn me into a dark blonde overall.

Afterwards he cuts a good four inches of damaged hair off. By the time he is finished I am totally confused. I don't look like myself, but I can see that the creature in the mirror is attractive. With soft tendrils around her mouth, drawing attention to its glossy color.

It's... It's, well, I guess, it's quite...sexy. I look sexy. Lana comes up to me, meets my eyes in the mirror. She smiles and nods her head.

'You'll do,' she says with great satisfaction, and I know it is the highest compliment I could receive from anyone. Because the truth is I don't just secretly hate her, I also secretly admire her.

Eight

It is the eve of the wedding. Tom comes to pick Billie and me up and drives us to the church for the rehearsal. Made of ancient grey stone it has a quaint feel to it. We are introduced to India Jane, the wedding organizer. She has a posh voice, no-nonsense eyes, and oozes superficial charm from every pore. As soon as everyone arrives she sets about taking us through our paces with impressive efficiency, but I am too excited to pay much attention to any proceedings that do not directly involve me. Tomorrow I will see Jack again! I try to picture that moment and wonder what he will make of my dream dress, and the new me.

I hardly speak to Lana as Blake never lets her out of his sight. I do, however, meet Blake's sister. A fully-grown, handsome woman who smiles artlessly, and behaves like a child. In the procession, she walks with a basket of flowers behind the flower girls and baby Sorab, who is carried in by his Nanny. He is given a dummy ring pillow to clutch.

I also meet all the groomsmen except for the best man who apparently has been through his part separately as he is attending a funeral wake. I wonder what it must be like to attend a funeral one day and a wedding the next.

At the end of it all, when Billie and I are about to get into the Bentley to be driven to Wardown Towers, where we will spend the night, Lana runs up to us and gives us devastating news.

I did do some research and discovered that Wardown Towers houses one of the largest and most fabulous art collections in private hands and is considered the grandest estate in Bedfordshire. It even has its own Zoo, but I go to it heavy-hearted and saddened. It is all for nothing.

Jack is not coming to the wedding.

The Wedding

Nine

It is 10.00 a.m. and I am in Wardown Towers. Billie and I spent last night here, because in four hours Lana will become Mrs. Blake Law Barrington. I have left them in the room with the make-up artist and the hairdresser while I go down the impressive curving staircase and walk through the many reception rooms and out into the stone courtyard. Stretched out below me is the vista of beautifully manicured gardens and farther away, but still part of the estate, the best and greenest of English countryside.

I watch workers stream like ants in and out of a large white marquee. They are carrying mostly flowers and plants, but also trays and boxes of all kinds. I go towards it and stand at the entrance.

Inside, it is bustling with activity.

A very gay man, presumably the one Lana says is from Beverly Hills, is prancing around giving orders. I gaze around in wonder. The tent is in the process of being turned into a gold, black and cream wonderland. The ceiling of the interior is made with hundreds of yards of crushed black velvet and looks like a giant black scallop. Fairy lights illuminate its whorls. Six enormous, three-tiered chandeliers hang from this sumptuously decadent ceiling.

The stage at the end of the room is made of hedge and surrounded by magnolia trees that were separated into trunks, branches and flowers so they could be flown in from America. Workers are reassembling them with staple guns. For a moment, the florist in me feels for those beautiful trees that will, after this one occasion lasting no more than a few hours, wither and die. The gratuitous waste of these beautiful trees is shocking. And yet this what I have read about in all the celebrity mags and longed to be part of. They are only trees, I tell myself. Raised solely for this purpose. Their greatest moment is here. When they are part of the fantasy garden a billionaire banker pays to create for his bride. She wanted a spring garden wedding.

She's got it.

I let my gaze wander over to the walls, made of billowing cream drapes, greenery swags and countless—and I mean countless—white flowers. The amount of flowers and leaves on the walls superseded only by the number of flowers on the three long dining tables that edge the room. I reach for one of the roses and lightly squeeze it. You can always tell the difference between the high and low quality ones by doing so. This is a high quality one.

Dinner is to be a plated meal and all the tables are already set with plates, cutlery and glasses. The centerpieces are tall, elegant candelabras entwined with trailing exotic flowers. They are surrounded by clusters of small, unlit candles.

Later I will see the real effect.

The middle of the room, meant to serve as a large dance area, is covered in a cream and gold carpet. There is no gift table because Lana and Blake have requested their guests to pledge donations either to CHILD or to their favorite charities. To the left of me is a long table where there are earplugs in cream boxes for when the music gets too riotous, a phone charging station, comfy slippers for feet tired of high heels on the dance floor, miniature bottles of sunscreen, bug repellent, paper fans, and cozy wraps for the women in case there is a sudden evening chill.

The attention to detail is astonishing.

I leave the tent and head back towards the room where the three of us are getting ready. I open the door. Billie is sitting in a toweling robe having her make-up done and Lana, who has already had her make-up done, is now having her hair styled. My hair is already done.

The videographer is filming and a photographer is clicking away.

'You're next,' the make-up artist says to me.

'OK,' I reply and go sit on a chair beside a window.

Fat Mary comes into the room and closes the door behind her. She is wearing a peach dress and a matching hat. For a change she actually looks all right.

'Cor blimey...have you girls seen the best man?' she asks and chortles.

'Vann Wolfe?' Lana asks with a laugh.

Mary indulges in a long whistle. 'Even his name is perfection. One look at him and I know he is going to be a fantastic lover.'

'How can you tell?' I ask curiously.

'Listen, love, I've been to bed with enough men to know who's going to whip it out, whip it in and wipe it, and who's got the slooooow hand and dazzling moves.'

I stare at her without comprehension. What the hell is a slooooow hand? I have only been with three guys and all three times it was a total and complete disaster. I was drunk, they were drunk. First time I was sixteen and he didn't even use a condom. He promised he would withdraw before he came and he didn't. He apologized, but what a bastard! What he did afterwards was unforgivable. Fortunately, that didn't end with an STD or a nine-month bump for me.

The second time it was three years later. I was at a party. He was confident, the way Jack was, but he had a big nose. He put his finger into my knickers and poked me when I wasn't expecting it. It was painful. I was drunk so he got on top and went for it. He said having sex with a condom on was like sucking a sweet with a wrapper still on it, but he didn't want no squalling baby. He wanted to spray his semen on my stomach. So he did. It was sticky and messy and I hated it. He tried to ask me out again, but I refused.

The next guy was at a club. I was very drunk. He was the deejay. He took me around the back and pushed his hard length against me. It was exciting. I had a condom in my purse and we used it, but afterwards I was still ashamed. I felt as if I had betrayed Jack. I know it sounds crazy but that's how I felt.

Fat Mary goes to sit on the bed and looks at Lana. 'So who is he?'

'His...father used to...work for Blake's family,' Lana explains, but I did not miss the pause before father and work.

'In what capacity?'

'His father was the butler. But Blake and Vann are very close. They grew up together so they are as close as brothers.'

'What does he do now?'

'I think he's trying to be an artist. He lives in Paris.'

All I hear is 'trying to be' and I decode that as poor. Church mouse poor.

'Oooo what I wouldn't do for one night with his steaming flesh,' purrs Fat Mary.

Lana laughs. 'You could be in luck, Mary. Blake tells me he likes the fuller figured woman.'

'That's sealed Grandview's fate for tonight, then,' she says in such a black widow spider voice that we all laugh.

'You are a terrible slut,' says Billie.

'Slut is so harsh. Dragon on the hunt is more appetizing.'

There is a knock on the door. Still laughing, Billie goes to open it.

'Hi,' she says, but her voice is suddenly different. We all turn towards the door.

'Hi,' a man's voice says and I feel my heart stop.

Oh! my God! Oh my God! The man standing at the door is none other than my Jack.

My stomach does a backflip. I swallow hard and compose my face. Billie opens the door wider and I see him framed in the doorway. I have never seen him in a suit, and, oh boy, he is so incredibly handsome he dazzles my eyes. But on closer examination he is Jack and yet he is not. The African sun has turned him as brown as a berry, but it is his eyes. They are dull and sad. Has he seen what he shouldn't have in Africa?

I have never been able to forget that time waiting at the dentist and, having read all the magazines on offer, picking up something on photography. Skimming through it bored me out of my skull, and coming upon that iconic picture of the sickly skeletal child crawling on the dusty, barren landscape towards a help center. Behind the child, a vulture following on foot, waiting for it to die. I researched the photographer on the net later, and it didn't shock me when I learned that he eventually took his own life.

Jack's eyes zero in on Lana. She stands up, her hand clamped on her mouth. For a moment no one moves and then she is flying across the room towards him, but instead of lunging into his arms as I have sometimes seen her do, she stops two feet away from him. There it is, the tension that Lana and Billie were discussing in the restaurant. Did they fall out?

'Hello, Lana,' he says. His voice is the same.

'You came,' Lana whispers. Her hand is pressed to her stomach.

'Of course. I did promise to give you away,' he says, and smiles. And for just one moment he seems as he was before.

'Oh!' Lana's face falls. She bites her lower lip. 'I'm sorry, Jack, but you never replied to any of my emails. I thought you weren't coming. Billie's father is giving me away,'

He shakes his head slowly. 'No he's not. I am. This is a surprise from Blake.'

It is only then that I realize that he is dressed in the color scheme chosen for the wedding. A blush-colored square of handkerchief is sticking out of his breast pocket. That little piece of material unifies his attire with mine.

Lana flings her arms around his neck joyfully. 'Oh, Jack. You almost ruined my wedding.'

His arms go around her. She lifts herself up on her toes and kisses his cheek. 'I'm so glad you're here. So glad. Thank you, thank you so much for coming.'

'I'll always be here for you.'

Lana sniffs.

'Don't spoil your make-up,' cries the make-up lady in a panic.

'I guess I'd better leave and let you finish getting dressed. I'll come back for you when you're ready.'

Lana disengages herself from him. He throws a quick glance at the rest of us in the room. 'Ladies,' he says, and then he is gone.

Lana looks at Billie. 'Did you know?'

'Of course,' Billie admits airily.

Lana goes to her mobile and calls Blake. All she says is, 'Thank you.'

I don't get to hear what he says, but her reply is rather intriguing as she says in a perfectly serious tone, 'I consider that sexual blackmail.' Then she turns around and goes back to sit in front of the mirror. She looks like the happiest bunny in the field. When she catches my eyes, she grins like a cat that has got the cream.

By the time the hairdresser puts the last wave into Lana's hair I am made up, coiffeured and dressed. Billie and I stand around and watch while the hairdresser carefully attaches Lana's mother's tiara in her hair. It is a cheap thing, a little tarnished, but the hairdresser is clever, fills it with tiny babies breath so it looks romantic and dreamy. We help Lana get into the dress. It looks even more gloriously beautiful now that her hair and face have been done up. Carefully the girl fits the veil onto Lana's head.

'You look good enough to eat,' says Billie.

'Wish Mum was here.'

Billie smiles and carefully lifts the veil over her face. The photographer clicks away. It is a beautiful moment.

Then Jack comes in. 'Are you ready?' he asks.

Lana nods.

'You look amazing. I'm so proud of you. Blake's one lucky man,' he says, but, even though he is smiling, his eyes are forlorn.

I pick up the bride's bouquet—it is made solely from calla lilies—and put it into Lana's hands.

'Time I was going,' I say, my voice all sugar and cinnamon, but nobody looks at me. I exit without Jack having even noticed I was there.

Later. My time will come later.

Ten

The bride is on her way. I didn't get into the same car as Billie, Lana and Jack. I left earlier, came in another. There are expensive chauffeured cars parked all the way up the road. I run up the steps of the church just to have a quick peek inside at the beautiful people. See if I can recognize any celebrities. The sound of violins playing drifts out of the entrance.

The church is the fruit that the tree of money bore. Even I, who have voraciously consumed hundreds of images of glamorous weddings, am startled by what big money can buy.

Overnight, the nave has been transformed into a fantasy garden. All the bays are filled with clusters of magnolia trees and every pew is festooned with greenery swags. The tropical liana vines entwined with flowers and leaves that droop down from the vaulted ceiling give the illusion that the aisle is a garden path. The ground is carpeted with green turf and scattered with flower petals. Hedges surround the altar.

Ah! That's where the forty thousand roses flown in from Ecuador and Holland at a cost of £125,000 ended up. The back of the church has become the most astonishing rose wall out of which the crucifix looms. I touch a stone pillar, now a luxuriously thick cylinder of flowers, and think of the symbol of the crucifix: nails pounding flesh and fiber into wood.

The pews are full of marshmallow-colored hats and morning suits, but since it is impossible to recognize anyone from the back, I go back outside to wait for Lana's arrival. I am standing on the top step when the cream Rolls-Royce draws up.

Oh, Lana!

How lucky you are.

Jack gets out first then Billie exits out of the far side. Jack comes around and helps Lana out and Billie picks up her train and holds it in her hands. The sun is shining on them and I realize that these are the people I have grown up with. In an unexplainable, funny, not ha ha way I love them all.

I go down the steps towards them. Lana's breathing seems wrong, all jerky and light, and Billie tells her, 'Try not to be a dick. Keep to the plan.'

Which seems to do the trick and makes Lana smile nervously. My Jack offers her the crook of his arm, and Billie gently spreads the train out on the ground so it is like a white bit of cloud trailing her.

India Jane beckons with her hands and as rehearsed the nanny comes forth with Sorab.

I'm not really into babies, but this kid looks edible in a mini tux. The pretty flower girls take their place in front, and Blake's sister, who seems barely able to contain her excitement, takes her place behind the flower girls. A man in a dark suit speaks into his walkie-talkie and gives the go-ahead signal.

'Ready?' Jack asks.

Unable to speak, Lana nods. Well, I don't know if she is really unable to speak but I am sort of projecting what I would be feeling if I were her. I see her take a deep breath. Billie gets behind Lana, I get in front of Lana and we are off. As we practiced at the rehearsal.

I walk down the aisle to the strains of *Canon in D*, head up, but tense and conscious of all the eyes on me. I'm not cut out to be the center of attraction. I take my place and sigh with relief. That went well. I swivel my head to look at Blake and I catch the eyes of the best man, the one who could not attend the rehearsal because he was attending the wake, the failed artist, and the one who Fat Mary reckons has a slooooooow hand and has nicknamed Grandview. He stands as tall as Blake and his straight shoulder-length sandy hair is in a ponytail. I disapprove of men with long hair. Lazy hippies.

He winks suddenly. At me!

For some seconds I am so surprised, I stare back at him. Then the bridal processional, *Prince of Denmark's March (Trumpet Voluntary)* by Jeremiah Clarke, fills the church and, without acknowledging him in any way, I tear my gaze away from him and towards the entrance.

The bride has arrived at the top step. All heads turn. Gasps and murmurs of approval rise from the seated guests. Truth is, every gasp and seal of approval is deserved. Some women are born to be brides. Lana is one of them. She pauses a moment, a vision in white, before slowly walking down the aisle.

I turn to look at Blake. He has made no concession to any sort of decorum. No surreptitious backward glances, no politely waiting for the bride to arrive by his side—instead he has completely turned his back to the altar and is watching Lana's progress down the aisle with a rapt expression. Like a rock that has been struck by the sun for such a long time that its skin starts to radiate warmth, his entire being radiates love. There is a soaring innocence in his intensity. And pride. Such pride. He reminds me of a mustang that has not been broken.

When she reaches him, Jack carefully lifts her veil, kisses her lightly on one cheek and, relinquishing her, moves back. Away from her. He is finally free of her. My heart leaps. One day he will be mine.

The rest of the ceremony is a blur.

It all happens, but the events strike me as scraps from a dream. So long awaited and then it slips through your hand like so much sand. Lana whispering, 'I do.' Blake possessively slipping a ring onto her third finger because—I read somewhere—of an ancient Greek belief that a vein from that finger goes directly to the heart. The kiss, an extravagant gesture that stretches and exposes the length of Lana's throat and makes me think of: ownership. Then it is over. The bride and groom are departing hand in hand down the aisle. Outside, we pose for photographs. I try to move closer to Jack.

My plan is foiled by a posh voice.

'The celebration will continue down the road, six miles from here,' she announces, a militaristic twinkle in her eyes. I can totally picture her deftly separating someone's head from their shoulders with a machete, wiping the blood off her hands and calmly sitting down to a round of wedding cake tasting.

Eleven

The fine guests have been herded to the lawn where they are sipping vintage pink bubbly, nibbling on canapés on the lawn while waiting to be called into the marquee by the ushers. There is a quartet playing. I put down the classy monogrammed cocktail napkin and my drink at the bar, and go back into the house. I smile to and run past the human wall guarding the staircase. Upstairs, I don't go to the bedroom I stayed in last night, or the room where we all got ready. Instead I go to the room Lana stayed in. I try the door and, to my surprised delight, it opens.

I slip in and shut the door. I look around the room. The bed is made. On the bedside table lies what appears to be some sort of journal. Immediately, I go to it. I open it and recognize Lana's flowing hand and flick through the pages quickly. I open it to a page at random. At the top there is a quotation. I begin to read it:

We build our temples for tomorrow,
strong as we know how,
And we stand on top of the mountain
free within ourselves.
        —Langston Hughes

When I came back from the church, Blake was awake. He must have heard the car in the driveway. He was standing in the living room waiting for me. There were bluish shadows under his eyes and my heart went out to him. He smiled faintly, as if he did not know how to react to me. I went up to him and laid my cheek on his chest. He had had a shower and he smelt clean and fresh. He nuzzled my hair.

'I woke up and found you gone,' he said.

'Did you think I'd run away?'

'You can never run away from me, Lana. I would journey into the underworld to find you. You are mine.'

'I went to church.'

'Yes, Brian said. I thought you didn't believe in God.'

'For short there is tall, for sad there is happy. For dark there must be light. I wanted to align myself with the God of goodness. I wanted to ask his help.'

'Oh, Lana. You and all the believers of this world. You pray and you pray and all your billions of unanswered prayers are like wailing cries somewhere. Your God doesn't exist.' His voice is so sad.

'How do you know?'

'Because if he did the world wouldn't be the way it is. And even if he does exist he is definitely not the lord of this world.'

I looked up into his face. Already the weight of being the head of the Barrington dynasty is changing the shape of his face.

'Why do you say that?'

89

'Look around you, Lana. The entire planet, land, air and sea, has been poisoned by sheer greed, your food is toxic, you are governed by sociopaths who wage war after war with impunity while promising peace, and humanity itself is poised on the brink of extinction. Who do you think is in charge? Your God of love and light, or mine?'

My eyes suddenly fly off the page. Footsteps. I freeze. Coming this way. Shit. I snap shut the book and look around me. Nearer. I dare not slip under the bed for fear of ruining my dress. I run to the wardrobe. Dresses. Lana's. I step into it and pull the door behind me, but even before I can click it shut, the door to the room opens and Lana and Blake enter. I close the door very, very slowly until there is but an inch left open. I say a little prayer that they will have no reason to open the cupboard. I find I can watch them through the little slit.

'Well, what's the surprise then?' asks Lana. There is a happy note in her voice. The happiness is surreal after what I read in her journal. There, she had been confused and unhappy, very unhappy.

'I've got a dress for you.'

'A dress?' she repeats. She seems surprised.

'Mmnnn.'

'What type of dress?'

'It's in the wardrobe, I'll get it,' he says and starts walking toward me.

Shit, shit, shit. I squeeze shut my eyes. I'll tell them I came in here by mistake. I was looking for the toilet.

And then he goes to the door of the other wardrobe. I take a deep breath. My heart is thudding like crazy. Thank God I chose this cupboard and not the other. I see him go towards Lana. The dress is in a green plastic covering. He holds it in front of her.

'Go on, take a look.'

'OK.' She unzips it and gasps at its content. Her eyes fly up to his face. One hand covers her mouth. 'There was only one in the shop, where did you get it from?' she asks.

He doesn't answer immediately. Instead he carefully takes the dress out of its covering. The dress is white with a Mandarin collar, three jewel-encrusted leaf-shaped cut-outs in the chest and slits up the side.

'Where did you get it from?' Lana repeats.

'I dug the other one out of the bin and told Laura I wanted an exact copy made. Exact material, exact color, exact thread, exactly the same stones, and if there was a missed stitch in the original, I wanted that copied too. They had to go to Paris to find the material.'

Lana laughs, surprised, but at the same time pleased. 'God! How much did it cost?'

'You don't want to know.'

'I can't believe you went to all that trouble.'

'You wrote in your journal that you loved it. And I was sorry the moment I tore it. You looked so beautiful that night.'

'Oh, darling. How I love you,' she says, her voice breaking. She starts fanning her face with her hands. 'You're going to make me spoil my make-up.'

Blake puts the dress on the bed and reaches out for her. She fits perfectly against his body.

'I've got a surprise for you too, but you can only have it tonight,' she says.

'Oh yeah? What is it?'

'It's a surprise.'

'You know I don't like surprises. They make me anxious.'

'This is a good surprise.'

'Do you want to see me suffer on my wedding day?'

'All right,' she relents. 'I'll give you one clue. If you don't get it you'll just have to suffer.'

'Go on then.'

'Deep.'

'Throat,' he says smugly.

She hits his chest and he laughs. 'Oh, you spoilsport. I hope you're happy now that you've ruined your wedding night surprise.'

'Where did you learn to do that?'

'Billie and I went to special classes in London.' She looks meaningfully at him.

'Billie wanted to learn how to deep throat?'

'Yeah, she said she'd always wanted to swallow a sword.'

Blake laughs and I am struck by how suddenly young and full of life he appears. 'That girl is incorrigible. What happened to her muscled guy?'

'Don't know. He said he'd call after a month, but he never did. Turned out it was just a one-night stand.'

'Shame. She liked him, didn't she?'

'Yeah,' Lana says thoughtfully, 'she did.'

'She'll find someone else. Anyway, I've got a wedding night surprise for you too.'

'Well, what is it?'

'I'm not telling and spoiling the surprise.'

'What? You made me spoil mine.'

He laughs wickedly.

'Give me one word.'

'Chocolate.'

'White, milk or dark.'

'Dark.'

'But I don't like dark.'

'You're not the one who will be doing the eating.'

Laughter gurgles through Lana. 'Oh! You predator.'

'I can't help it when I scent easy prey.'

'Easy prey!' Lana huffs. 'I'll get you for that later. Let's go. People will start to think we are up to something.'

'Let them. Stay with me another minute.'

There is laughter in her voice. 'OK, but just a minute.'

'What kind of underwear are you wearing?'

'White as the driven snow, tiny, frothy and with ribbons trailing down my thighs. It made even my head reel to look at them.'

'Quick peek?'

'Let's not add sticky to the list of adjectives, shall we?'

'How about if I only use my teeth on the ribbons?'

'How about if I put you over my knee and spank you?'

He throws his head back and roars with laughter, the sound masculine, rumbling from deep within. 'That'll be the day, Mrs. Barrington.'

When he stops she put her hands on either side of his face and kisses him lightly on the lips. 'Oh, Blake. You've made today so special.'

He kisses her ear. 'No, it is you who has made today special. Today, Mrs. Blake Law Barrington, I'll even put up with that ear technique Billie taught you.'

'Go ahead and laugh. I learned things in London. You'll be gagging for my techniques.'

'I'm already begging now.' He bends his head to her neck and whatever it is he does makes her gasp. 'Stop. You're turning me on.'

'How 'bout a quickie, hmmm? I've never had it off with a married woman before.'

Lana steps back and slaps his hands down. 'Behave or I will have to tell my husband.'

'And what will you tell him, Mrs. Barrington?'

'I will tell him I met an irresistible man who tried to seduce me with promises of chocolate, but I didn't succumb.'

'I wish all these people would go home.'

'Come on, let's get back to the party.'

'All right,' he agrees reluctantly.

They are already at the door when Lana notices her journal.

'Wait,' she says, 'I'd better lock this away. I wouldn't want anybody accidentally reading about all the things we get up to.'

'You're going to need a new book halfway through our honeymoon,' he teases as she puts it into the drawer, locks it and drops the key into his trouser pocket. They close the door and leave and I wait until their footsteps die away before I creep out of the cupboard.

Wow, wow, wow!

First off, I thought Billie was a lesbian. What's she doing having one-night stands with muscular men? And Billie and Lana taking lessons in sexual techniques? Deep throat. Chocolate? And that strange diary that Lana is keeping. His God and her God... What could it all mean?

I wish I had had the chance to read more. I try the drawer, but it is definitely locked. I go to the bed and touch the white dress. The material is soft and smooth. I hold the dress up. It is so beautiful. I have never had anything so fine and probably never will. Again I suffer that old sharp, swift twist of envy. It is a demon that will not lie down and sleep or die.

I open the door, dart down the corridor, take the small staircase at the back, and cross over to the long corridor that leads to the vegetable gardens. From there I run along the high brick wall and, sprinting to the marquee, I slip in through the staff entrance. I walk to my table under the disapproving stare of India Jane and slip into my seat.

'Where have you been?' mutters Fat Mary.

'I had an emergency.'

'Nice one,' Billie comments, as the music lowers and the Master of Ceremonies announces, 'Ladies and gentlemen, please join me in welcoming Mr. and Mrs. Blake Law Barrington.'

We all rise to our feet and clap to welcome the beautiful couple. After their entrance, not much worthy of note occurs until after the starters of tender lamb brochettes with honey roast shallot have been dispensed with.

Then the best man stands and begins his speech. 'I'll try to keep this short,' he says lazily, 'since I wouldn't want to intrude in that cherished but brief period between 'I do' and 'You'd better.'

The guests break out in laughter. But the thing about him is he really means it. After complimenting the bride and bridesmaids and thanking us he wraps up with the words. 'I'd like to propose a toast: to Lana and Blake! May the rest of your lives be filled with joy, wonder, laughter and love.'

We all raise our glasses.

Twelve

I notice her immediately. It could be because she has that same regal bearing and inbred disdain of all those fortunate women that grace the pages of *Hello*! An air that I immediately admire and gravitate towards. I see her snap her fingers at a waiter bearing a tray. When he veers to her, she picks up a glass of red wine from his tray and, without taking a sip from it, begins to walk towards me. It is only when she is maybe ten feet away from me that I realize: she is not striding purposefully towards me, but towards Lana.

I heard Blake excuse himself a few minutes earlier to go to the Men's room and Lana is talking to a blonde woman who is congratulating her. The woman seems a little drunk. I hear the laughter in Lana's voice as the woman leans into her. I turn back to look at the socialite bearing the glass of red wine. She is only a few feet away and the expression on her face chills me. There is so much hatred and loathing etched in it. And everything happens too quickly for me to comprehend.

I hear Lana gasp. There is fear in that sound. The socialite is already standing between her and the tipsy woman. In a flash I know exactly who she is. This is Cleopatra and the serpent all rolled into one; this is the ex who has been watching Lana from afar. Victoria!

True, I am envious of Lana and of all the things she has, but at that moment, through a process I do not understand, she becomes my friend. I know instinctively that she is in danger and my first thought is to protect her. I know I should do something, and I want to, but I am frozen to the spot. I don't know how to be brave. I have never been in my life.

The socialite's eyes glint dangerously. She is like a living switchblade. 'You think you are so clever. But you have no idea what you've caught in your little net. He has done what they all have to do... Things that will make your skin crawl.'

'No, he's not like the rest of you,' Lana whispers, but her voice is full of horror.

Victoria's response is instant. Like a dagger. From her mouth into Lana's heart. 'Is it possible that you are truly that blind or are you just a willfully stupid cunt?'

The movement is fast, confused. There is a sudden blur of flesh. She jerks her wine glass upward, and red liquid flies out in a graceful arc— no, no, not the beautiful dress—and splashes onto Lana's dress. The glass falls to the carpet, rolls away soundlessly.

You fucking animal, I want to scream, but I am too shocked and horrified to react, and so, it appears, is Lana. The attack is so sudden, so unexpected. Lana is just standing there white-faced and paralyzed, even as the devil woman, her face twisted with homicidal rage, raises her arm and lets it smash down towards Lana's face. But the strike splicing the air never reaches. A man standing nearby, who had earlier simply seemed to me to be a slightly inebriated guest, suddenly and with lightning speed catches the slap mid-air.

He twists her body against his own, as she struggles and kicks ineffectively in his vise-like arm lock. At that moment she looks as repulsive as any slimy bug you would find wriggling under a wet stone. Even in the large man's grip, Victoria never takes her eyes off Lana. Her features contorted, and hissing like a venomous snake, she pushes her face forward. A spray of spittle falls across Lana's cheek. They stare at each other. The concentrated, utter hatred is shocking.

'You don't know him. You can *never* know him,' she enunciates coldly and clearly, her eyes glittering triumphantly, even as the man begins to drag her away.

Lana simply stares at her, her mouth slack with shock, as if she cannot comprehend the viciousness of the other woman. Her hands are visibly trembling. At that moment for the first time in my life I feel sorry for her. All these people staring at her humiliation with the same mixture of pity and horrified curiosity of people who slow down at car crashes to watch.

Poor Lana. Her beautiful wedding has been utterly ruined. And the dress that she had loved so much is surely beyond redemption. I remember her saying, 'I'll store it carefully in case my daughter wants to wear it some day.'

Another man in a suit, but obviously part of the security service too, runs up to help and the bitch is bodily picked up and carted away. That is when she screams something that stills my heart and makes the hairs at the back of my neck rise.

'He has blood on his hands. Children's blood,' she screeches maniacally.

Her words seem to slam into Lana. She flinches and sways on her feet.

'One day I will kill you,' is the last thing Victoria screams before she starts venting her fury at the men who are dragging her away. 'Let go of me, you fucking, ugly cunt. Take your filthy hands off me right now. Do you know who I am?' She is still hurling abuse and insults when she is dragged outside, with a hand probably clamped over her mouth.

Nobody moves. The tension in the room is so palpable that the music suddenly seems overly loud and jarring. Another 'guest' detaches himself from the frozen milieu of people and goes up to Lana. His eyes are watchful and hard.

'Are you all right?' he asks. His voice is soft and kindly, at odds with the cold light in his eyes.

Lana nods mutely, and as soon as the best man appears beside Lana, he nods again, and goes the way of the other men and their struggling captive.

Vann Wolfe puts his arm around Lana's shoulders and looks down at her, kindness in his eyes. From the corner of my eyes I see Billie start running towards Lana. She looks utterly furious. There is a white line around her mouth. But she comes to a sudden standstill, and when I look to where her gaze is, I see Blake striding towards Lana.

His eyes are terrifying and his jaw is clenched so hard the muscles in his neck are rigid. I will never forget that look of unbreakable purpose as long as I live. There is no one else in the room for him. Only Lana. When he reaches her, the best man falls back, and she raises her shocked eyes up to him.

'She'll never stop, will she?' she gasps. Her eyes are large and wounded.

'No harm can befall a single hair on your head while I am alive,' he tells her tenderly. The deep love he has for her is unmistakable. It shines in his eyes, radiates out of his being.

Tears fill her eyes.

At the sight of her tears even the backs of my own eyes start stinging. The awfulness of what has happened is impossible to describe. How wrong it had all gone in the blink of an eye. I thought back to how happy she had been while we were all getting ready this morning.

'My dress—' she whispers hoarsely.

'Can be recreated to the last stitch. Remember...' he reminds so gently, I am startled. How could a man with such cold, hard eyes be so utterly gentle and tender? It seems inconceivable. I watch transfixed as he simply gazes into her eyes and something deep and secret seems to pass between them. A something that I have never known. A look of belonging. The tears that were brimming in her eyes spill over. With one finger he gently wipes first one cheek and then the other.

'Thank God for waterproof mascara,' he says.

Must be some private joke, because Lana sniffs and smiles weakly.

'That's my baby,' he says, and raises a hand almost like a child asking the teacher for permission to be excused. In fact it is a cue. Suddenly all the light cuts out except for the twinkling lights that look like diamonds in the velvet blackness of the ceiling. Two spotlights come on and, searching the room, find them.

Lana looks surprised.

In the darkness comes the disembodied, honeyed, deeply baritone voice of Barry White, *'We got it together, didn't we?'* And that sexy guffaw he had.

After that a sound like rushing water, then another like a didgeridoo, a vibrating haunting sound, and then the keys of a piano are tinkled... I know this song... Of course... Rihanna's unmistakable, silky voice cuts through the dark, 'Shine bright like a diamond.'

Inside the spotlights, Blake curls one large hand around Lana's delicate hand and his other hand goes to rest on the small of her back, and then he is whirling her around and they are dancing their first dance, a beautifully choreographed paso. Their movements so perfectly matched it's like a real life *Come Dancing*.

No one speaks. No one moves. Everybody is staring at the splendid sight of two very beautiful people dipping and whirling round and round the dance area. Their movements fluid, effortless, perfectly matched and undeniably majestic.

He raises her in the air. Time stops. The notes hold, shimmer, she is returned to the ground; they glide along, moving as if they are one body, two people making graceful, magical circles. Blake twirls Lana and while she is spinning he catches her and kisses her. I stare at the sight. It is not possible to describe the beauty of that moment, that dance. Then the dance is over, and as if released, the crowd comes alive and spontaneously breaks into applause.

I tear my eyes away from the couple and look for Jack. I find him and my heart stops in my chest. Irish is standing frozen across the dance floor, his face a mask of terrible longing. His eyes are trained on the kissing couple. He is still madly, deeply, head over heels in love with Lana. The unfairness of it hits me like a blow in the gut. I actually experience pain at the core of my body.

Three spotlights hit the stage and—oh my God—it is Rhianna standing in the bright lights, a star in a tight sequined costume clapping and smiling. The crowd gasps and goes wild with pleasure and surprise.

'Yeah, it's me,' she says and laughs.

She holds her hand out in the direction of Lana and Blake. 'I dropped in to congratulate the new couple. Give a hand, everybody, to Mr. and Mrs. Blake Law Barrington.'

Everybody claps and cheers. I turn to look at Lana's face and she has her hand over her mouth, but not with horror—delight. She had not known. Blake has his arm around her waist and is looking at her indulgently. At that moment Lana is no longer the humiliated bride at her own wedding. Just by the simple act of raising his hand the billionaire banker has turned everything around. She is once again wearing the coveted shoes that every woman wants to be in.

'Thank you,' Rihanna shouts into the mic. 'Shall we get this party on the road?'

'Yeah,' the guests reply.

'I don't think I heard that.'

'Yeah,' comes the louder, more definite reply back.

She makes the horned symbol to the crowd, six dancers surround her and begin gyrating as she starts her next number, *Don't Stop The Music*.

I look away from the stage and see Billie go up to Lana and Blake, and as if they have rehearsed this beforehand, Blake lets go of Lana and Billie links the fingers of her right hand through Lana's, and gently kissing her cheek leads her away from the marquee. From where I am standing their unshakable bond tweaks at my ancient envy. I damp it down. I guess they will be going back to the house so Lana can change. Perhaps she will change into that beautiful white dress with the jeweled cut-outs.

I turn my attention to Blake. To the stony expression on his face as he watches his wife leave with her friend. Someone comes up to him, says something and he inclines his head to listen, his eyes still on Lana. The poor guy is still talking to him when he strides away in the direction that Victoria has been dragged to, his mobile held to his ear. Beneath the tightly controlled man, an implacably angry, raging beast. This is not a man to cross.

I wish I could follow him and see what happens to Victoria. Will he slap her, the sound reverberating? I am electrified by the thought of that slap. It will be the slap that I wish I had delivered.

On stage Rihanna and her dancers are strutting their stuff. I scan the room. It is now full of dancing people. An elderly lady in a soft gray suit is dabbing her eyes and reaching for her box of earplugs.

I know I should have just left it. Let it go, but I couldn't. I go up to Jack. I wanted him to see and acknowledge the new me. Maybe if he saw the new me he might change his mind, slowly fall in love with me. I edge along the sides of the room until I am standing beside him.

Thirteen

'**H**i.'

He looks down at me, and for a split second I see a slash of annoyance, then recognition and genuine surprise. 'Julie?'

'Mmmm...' I gaze innocently at him from under my lashes, the way Lady Diana used to. I hope I come off as vulnerable and flirtatious as she used to.

'You look different.'

'Different better or worse?'

'Definitely different better.'

A fierce flash of pride and pleasure go through me at his words. My heart starts beating really fast. I am determined to have this man. 'I've got to talk to you. Come with me,' I say, and, grasping his arm, lead him into the corridor and down it. I open the first door to my right, look in—it is empty. I pull him in with me.

'What's up?'

I turn to close the door and my heart is in my throat. The room in semi-darkness with the drapes pulled halfway across the tall windows and two lit corner lamps. I am glad for it. My cheeks are burning up. In the dim of the soaring ceiling amongst the grand furniture, I try frantically to remember exactly what I had planned to say, and fuck me, nothing comes into my head.

My mind is blank.

I feel dread crawl up my spine as I turn to face him. He is looking at me curiously. I swallow hard. The blood is pounding so hard in my ears I hear it like a roar. All I can think of is how much I love him. I have loved this man for so long. I love everything about him. I love the bewilderingly silent pauses he lapses into. There will always be a part of him that can never be known, not by his mother, not by Lana and not by me. But I even love that he will never wholly be known.

I love the way he holds his jaw in that aggressive slant. I love the way everybody respects him. Or the way his hair is slicked back without any parting. And his tormented blue eyes. In my dreams they are hot and passionate. I laugh when he laughs. I love, love, love everything about this man. He has to love me back. In the end he must fall in love with me.

If only he would take me in his arms. If only there was no need for words. I squeeze my eyes shut. Where, oh where are the words that I have so carefully planned?

'Are you all right, Jules?'

Jack's voice cuts into my confused thoughts. I don't like to swear, but fuck, fuck, fuck, FUCK! My eyes snap open. His face is puzzled but interested.

'Yeah, I'm fine,' I gulp.

'What did you want to talk to me about?'

I open my mouth and close it again. Thousands of unfinished sentences pass through my empty head, each one as incoherent as the one that had gone before.

'What is it?' he repeats, this more urgently. He reaches out a hand and takes mine in it.

At the touch of his hand I begin to tremble violently. Oh my God, Oh my God, it is going to happen like it happens in my dreams. He is going to take me in his arms.

'Jules?' He takes a step closer, and it seems to me that his whole radiantly clean heart is concerned. Even in this dim light I know he can see how tense my body has become. I am a nervous mess.

I open my mouth. 'I love you,' I blurt.

The room becomes so deadly silent that I dread to expel the breath I am holding. He looks like a nine-year-old boy that has had a bra thrown in his face. The incredulity in his dear face would have had me rolling with laughter in different circumstances. He frowns. A quick flash of some emotion crosses his eyes. I cannot understand it. Before I can even properly register it in my mind or its implications, I am swamped with that famous Jack smile. The smile that made all the girls in school swoon. He does not drop my hand, but gallantly, and in an oddly old-fashioned gesture, raises it to his lips and kisses it.

'You will never be happy as the wife of a poor man.'

'But I love you.'

He lays his fingers on my mouth. 'One day you will find someone who is perfect for you, perhaps even the rich man of your dreams. And that day you will thank your lucky stars that nothing became of this day.'

I do not like the tone he has taken. This is wrong, all wrong. Even if he had said he loathed me it would be preferable, but this tone, as if I am a hurt child that needs to be soothed. I won't have it.

'She's married now. You can never have her. Have me, please.'

It is as if I have slapped him. He draws away from me. Never before have I seen so much misery in anyone's face except maybe that one time with my father.

'You have your love and I have mine,' he says sadly, and turns away to leave.

I grab his sleeve. 'Wait, Jack.'

He turns back. His voice is dull. 'I don't want to hurt you, Jules. Please, let's just pretend we never came into this room.'

'You can learn to love me.'

'I could never love you.'

My mouth drops open. Maybe later I will feel shame. Now I just know I must carry on. I have come this far. 'Yes, you can,' I insist stubbornly.

He shakes his head.

'How do you know?' I demand, my voice rising hysterically. 'You haven't even tried.'

He stares at me with that pitying look. He doesn't want me. He won't even give me a chance. Even if it is just to prove that I am not good enough for him. Somewhere in my brain a fire splutters and rises up. I gather up my dignity and let loose the rage of hurt pride. I will turn this into a liberating experience even if it kills me.

'I hope you're not waiting for her. Because Blake is never letting her go. You'll never have her,' I cry vindictively.

His face pales in the gloom. 'I am not waiting for her. I'm leaving tomorrow.'

'What? You arrived today and you're leaving tomorrow?'

'Yes, I am needed in Africa. I am not here.'

'You are needed here. I need you.'

'I am here to keep a promise to dance at Lana's wedding,' he says, and depressing the door handle, quietly leaves.

'Oh, you, you...' At that moment I cannot think of a word that is bad enough. My hands are clenched tight and my breath comes in hard bursts. 'Fool!' I holler at the closed door.

There's a chair nearby and I sink into it. The reaction to my wild outburst has made my knees weak. I feel so bewildered. He did not want me. Was it all for nothing then? I no longer feel furious, just a strange, cold emptiness. I place the palms of my hands against my humiliated cheeks.

Oh! The vile things I had said to him. He must hate me. Forever, I will be haunted by that stricken look on his face when I flung at him that he would never have Lana. How I regret those unkind words that I can never take back.

My eyes fall upon a painting of a seated crone in a thick white shawl, her deeply lined face enclosed in a full and heavily ribboned white cap. I look at her puckered mouth and for some insane reason it makes me want to scream.

'Damn it to hell, I've ruined it. I've lost him,' I wail, and, burying my face in my hands, mourn.

'Nothing drives a man away faster than desperation,' says a deep male voice from the depths of the gloomy room.

I spring up in startled confusion and whirl around in the direction of the voice.

Fourteen

The best man is hanging his head out from the side of a huge sofa. He has very white teeth, which gleam in the darkness. Shame runs up my throat and flames into my face. Can it get worse? Now Grandview has witnessed my total humiliation too.

'You were listening to a private conversation. You should have made your presence known,' I accuse angrily.

'I would have, but the conversation took a turn for the worse before I could announce my presence.' He says it reasonably enough, but his eyes are laughing at me.

'Oh! How dare you mock me?'

'I'm not mocking you. It just seems to me that you are going about your process of seduction the wrong way.'

For a moment I consider turning around and sailing out of the room, my head held high. But...in spite of myself I am intrigued. I march up to him.

'What do you mean?' I demand haughtily, looking down at him as disdainfully as you can to someone who has witnessed you make a complete fool of yourself in the most cringe-worthy way possible.

He gestures towards the high-backed chair opposite him, and I perch on him. I don't plan to stay long. Up close he has very strong features. He looks like one of those Australian surfer boys. It must be his light hair. Good-looking, I suppose, but nowhere near as fine as Jack. My Jack is so beautiful it sometimes hurts me just to look at him.

Fine wisps have escaped his ponytail, and hang about his face. He sits up and pushes them back. He places his fist on the armrest—it is full of golden hairs, and I am struck by its resemblance to a lion's paw. Not in the sense of shape but in sensation alone. It looks so cuddly, ineffective and harmless, and yet one swipe could rip out the contents of a man's belly. He has been lying stretched out on the sofa and has taken his shoes off.

'You have a hole in one of your socks,' I say.

He grins shamelessly. 'I left my knitting needles in Paris.'

A hippie and a smart Alec. Whatever. 'What did you mean just now when you said I was going about it the wrong way?'

'When outnumbered by the enemy, a stubborn or simple-minded man will fight face to face in the open until he is killed. A smart man will react differently. He will strategize, find the weakness of his opponent and exploit it. As in war so in love.'

The sexual encounter, they say, is a flowery battle between a man and a woman.'

'A flowery battle?'

He nods. 'Every night the last Emperor of the Manchu dynasty turned over an ornate jade name plaque next to his bedchamber and a new concubine from his stock of three thousand girls would be brought to his bed. In 1856 the Celestial Prince picked a plaque that carried the name Yehonala.'

Yehonala—a concubine called Yehonala. The idea is intriguing.

'As was the custom, the odalisque was carried on the back of a eunuch, covered only by a red silk sheet. He laid the twenty-one-year-old virgin at the foot of the bed, and to symbolize her complete subjection to the will of the Lord of Ten Thousand Years, she had to crawl on all fours towards him. All the naked girl had to become the mistress of her own fate was that one night.'

Grandview pauses. I lean forward. When he speaks again his voice is soft.

'One night with which to bewitch a dissipated god-king whose tastes were varied and, according to some, perverted. Beauty was of no use as every girl in the harem had been chosen for her good looks. Intelligence: he could find a hundred other scholars to discuss worldly affairs with. Humor: he had the Court's professional comedians.'

In spite of myself I am utterly fascinated. I strain to catch his words, to enter the foreign world he was weaving.

'No one knows what she did that first night, but whatever occurred was what the ambitious girl had learned during the five years that she had been languishing within the vermillion walls, virtually a prisoner, not a functioning man in sight, and while the Emperor was not even aware of her existence. She had tirelessly learned everything she could of the arts of love. Every closely guarded technique and all the secrets and practices of feminine allure became hers. That knowledge and sexual prowess made her irresistible to the pleasure-sated Emperor, and from that night on no one could usurp her place as the Imperial bed-partner. She let the Chinese poet Chang Heng speak again after two thousand years: "No joy shall be equal to the delights of this first night, these shall never be forgotten, however old we may grow."

'The Emperor became utterly besotted with her and remained so until his death. In that one night her skills set in motion the events that ultimately led to the collapse of the centuries-long Manchu reign and the rise of a woman to power. Yehonala claimed the throne and became China's last and most famous Empress. She became known as the She Dragon of China.'

Vann stops speaking and looks at me. My eyes travel down to his hands. They too are sprinkled with golden hairs. Big. Squarish. Well shaped. Masculine. Nice. Very nice. My mind goes blank. What the hell am I doing? I sit back, turn my voice disbelieving. 'How could a virgin with no previous sexual contact with a man do that?'

He smiles. 'Perhaps sex is not what you think it is?'

I frown. I am sixteen again, sore, the ejaculation leaking out of me. I remember he had gone out of the room and told his friends, 'Like fucking a pillow, man.' They had laughed. I had wiped myself and gone out, and pretended that I was not dying inside. The memory brings acute pain. I bow my head. 'Well, what is it then?'

'Sex is in the head.'

I frown.

'Here, let me demonstrate. Close your eyes and do not open them until I tell you to do so.'

I look at him carefully. He appears relaxed. He has not moved a fraction of an inch from his position on the sofa and does not appear inclined to do so. What harm can come from a little demonstration? I close my eyes.

'Imagine a white lotus bud. Do you know what a lotus looks like?'

I open my eyes and look at him, one eyebrow raised. 'I'm a florist.'

His lips lift upwards, his hand waves down. I close my eyes.

'Imagine that this lotus bud is very special. It can enter you...'

I squirm internally, a little, at that thought.

'I take the lotus by the stalk and I hold it against your forehead. Instantly your forehead opens to allow the tip and slowly the entire bud into it. I pull the lotus out and place it at the base of your throat. Once again your body opens and welcomes it in. I do the same to the middle of your chest. In and out. Slowly. Next your belly button. The lotus disappears into it and out again. Now it is poised over your pussy. I gently insert it inside. First the tip and then, as your body learns to accommodate it, the whole bud, even the widest part. It feels tight, but you can take it. I pull it out and now it is hovering over your anal cavity.'

I swallow hard but I don't allow my expression to change.

'The tip enters your ass. Slowly, because you are not used to it, I bury it deeper and deeper, until the whole thing has been swallowed up by your body.'

I open my eyes and put on a bored expression. 'And?'

'You are sitting in a puddle.'

I flush horribly. It is true. His voice, the strange environment, being spoken to like that by a total stranger.

'Sexual confidence is an allure that a man finds impossible to resist. Would you like to learn the arts of sex magick?'

I raise my head and look into his eyes. Lana and Billie have been learning to deep throat among other things. Above all else I want Jack. If Yehonala's way will do the job then so be it. 'Yes.'

'Good,' he says wolfishly. His name is very apt. Wolfe! I don't know how I did not notice it before.

He roots around his pocket and comes up with a pen.

'I don't normally carry one, but I was working on my best man's speech.' In another pocket he finds a folded piece of paper. 'Best man's speech,' he says and tears a small corner off. He writes on it.

'Twelve sessions, three times a week. Starting Monday at 7.00 p.m.,' he says and holds it out to me.

I take it. Our fingers touch and my hand sparks and tingles with the contact from his. That jolt shocks me, sends currents into my viscera. I withdraw quickly. It must be the static electricity from the layers and layers of organza in my dress. Confused, I hurriedly bend towards the paper in my hand. An address: Bread Street in London.

'How much will the…training cost?' There is a pause. Head bent, I am hanging on his words.

'My cock in that sulky little mouth of yours.'

My eyes rush up to meet his expression. He grins. Totally and utterly confident in his own skin. I feel the heat rushing into my cheeks. I feel dirty and horrified, but I am also transfixed and hooked. He and I will be having sex. But of course.

'Get a life,' Billie would say.

I have never done anything so outrageous in my life. Now is the time to back out. And yet I don't. I don't want to. I am strangely excited and turned on by the prospect of sex with this lion-man. I'm not with Jack yet. Besides I'm doing this for Jack. It is not different from Lana and Billie taking lessons on how to deep throat. Maybe he will teach me that too.

Bereft of any clever thing to say and unable to hold the strange intensity of his laughing eyes I drop my gaze to the scrap of paper and pretend to study the bold, slanting handwriting.

'Will you allow me to paint you?'

I raise my head, startled. 'You want to paint me?' I splutter.

His eyes are twinkling and his laugh is warm and sensual. 'Yes. A sulky mouth and slanting green eyes is a very unusual combination.' He moves his attention to my mouth.

I feel his gaze like a physical touch on my lips. There is an odd fluttering in my stomach. He did not impress me as much at first glance, but there is definitely something commanding about this man.

'My eyes are not green.'

'They are now.'

'Oh! Well, I guess I should be going,' I croak, and spring up, all flustered and hot. Should I warn him about Fat Mary? Nah... Let him suffer.

'See you Monday,' he calls, the laughter still ringing in his voice.

'See you Monday,' I throw over my shoulder, as I flee from the room where I was turned down by the love of my life, and was propositioned by a wolf! It is exciting. It is definitely exciting.

Fifteen

As a fun event India Jane has hired a fortune-teller to work the tables. I watch her nod to someone and make her way to our table. She is a parody of a gypsy, with a colorful scarf tied around her head, hoop earrings dangling down to her shoulders, a ruffled white blouse, a full skirt, red stockings and black shoes. Her complexion is swarthy, her nose is hooked and her eyes are beady and sly. They alight on me.

She advances and holds out a dark hand to me. Her gaze is unwavering and intense. Strange even. I don't want her to read my palm. I am the stealer of secrets and the hider of many. I swing my hand behind my back like a child and she smiles oddly.

Someone at the tables laughingly says, 'Come on, Julie, it's only a bit of fun.'

But her eyes bore steadily into mine, and there is not the least hint of fun in them as she wills me to submit. Like a hypnotized rabbit I hold my arm out to her. She captures my outstretched hand, turns it palm upwards and slowly brushes her other hand over it. Her palm is leathery. Her eyes release mine and move to my trembling hand.

'You will get him if you don't give up.'

I flush hard. She knows about Jack. She is about to spill my secrets. I knew I shouldn't have let her take my hand. I try to snatch it away, but she has it in an iron grip.

'I see you traveling with him... And children... Two girls. Very good man. Strong... Tall.' Her eyes narrow. 'Fatherless.' Then she frowns. Her deeply black eyes travel upwards to mine, a startled, almost fearful expression in them. 'Evil will try to tempt you, touch you. Don't let it.'

This time I pull my hand away and she allows me to.

'Now give me a coin, so you don't owe me anything,' she commands.

I stare at her. Her face is set in uncompromising lines. She has not asked for a coin from anyone else. I have no coins. I turn to the man sitting next to Billie. 'Can I have a coin please?'

He laughs, takes a coin from his wallet and holds it out to the gypsy. She shakes her head. 'It must come from her.' He passes it to me and I give it to her. The gypsy nods and moves on to the next table.

My heart is beating hard in my chest. I am so exhilarated I can hardly sit down. I press my tingling palms together and rub them. She said, if I do not give up I will get my Jack. Everything else she said fitted too. *Good. Tall. Strong. Fatherless.*

And she sees me traveling away with him. Does that mean I will be traveling to Africa? The prospect fills me with excitement. I do not understand her warning about evil so, as I have always done, I discount it as one unimportant inaccuracy in her prediction.

It is time for the happy couple to cut the tall, six-tiered cake—a holy smokes affair that has been patterned to look like the softly glowing painted glass shades of Tiffany lamps. It is so beautiful and unique it seems a shame to cut it. Anyway, they are cutting it, and I am not staying around to watch. Happy occasions always depress me.

I walk along the dozens of twinkling luminaria, over-sized white paper pom-poms and lanterns that flank the outdoor walkway towards the greenhouse. I just need to get away from the noise and joy of the party. I just need to think. About Jack and everything that has happened. About how I can win him back. I stand by the pond and look at the fishes glinting in the water. Do fishes sleep?

'Hey.'

I whirl around. It is Lana. In the soft light she looks very beautiful. Why has she followed me? She is the bride, the sparkling star of the party. The princess of the day.

'Are you all right?'

'Yes. Of course. Why do you ask?'

'You just looked a bit lost for a moment.'

That—and you know I don't like to swear—but that fucking gets my back up. I am *not* feeling lost. I laugh. The sound is unnatural. I curse it. 'No, I'm fine.'

'I think Vann likes you.'

Fuck you! I don't want Vann, I want Jack. I am so irritated and annoyed at that moment, I don't care that it is her day. She was the bride and all of us were meant to be the moons that orbit around her great body.

'Oh wonderful. Thank you so much. You kept the billionaire for yourself and saved the servant for me.'

Her conspiratorial smile turns into an O of shock. There is a hurt look in her eyes. Like a child that has been slapped when it came for a kiss. Shame punches through me. I am furious with myself. At that moment I hate myself. I am the worst bitch in the world. I fucking hate myself. I honestly did not mean to say that. I mouthed those ugly thoughts before I was conscious of them myself. I was just in my own world, my own wounded world. How I wish she hadn't followed me. How I wish I could take the words back.

We stare at each other.

There is a sound at the doorway. We both turn. Blake looks at us, his eyes going from one to the other, and then they rest briefly on me. I see the cold fury in them. He knows I have upset his doll, and he is intimidating as hell. Great, now I have pissed off the billionaire. No flat in Little Venice for me. Fuck them both. I raise my chin. I'm not about to apologize. But Lana does the good thing, the right thing. She comes to me and puts her hand on my arm. Her wedding ring is cool against my warm skin.

'I'm sorry. I shouldn't have interfered?'

For a moment I just look at her and feel truly outclassed and outgunned. She is the bigger person. She is trying to make it all OK again. Why? I don't know and I don't care. I lean forward and hug her. She is the thinnest person I have hugged. Come to think of it, I have never hugged anyone else but my mother, and that was many years ago, and even then my hands had not gone around all of her. We move away from each other. I fancy that she must be relieved to be drawing away.

'Let's have lunch when I get back,' she says.

I am too choked to speak. I simply nod.

'I actually came to give you this.' She hands me her bouquet.

I take it from her with both hands. The frog in my throat croaks out a thanks.

'Got to go. I'll call you when I get back.'

I know she is flying off to a surprise, secret location first, and Billie will be staying at Lana's apartment with Sorab, but after a week Billie and Sorab will fly out to Thailand to meet the couple for a week-long holiday.

'Yes, please do.'

She grins. 'Good, I'll bore you then with all my photographs.'

I smile weakly, and she turns away from me and goes to Blake. They link hands. I watch him.

His entire attention is on Lana. Without another glance at me, he takes her hand and guides her away from me, the super bitch. At the door Lana turns around.

'He's not who you think he is,' she says, and then they go down the lantern-lit path. I watch them walk under the fairy lights and the oversized pom-poms until they are swallowed by the topiary garden. But even from here I can already see the guests have lighted their sparklers. Hundreds are waving around. There is clapping and cheering and wedding bubbles start rising up. A beautiful end to a superb day. I wish I had not come here alone. I should have stayed with everyone else.

Suddenly music, music that I recognize booms out of the loudspeakers, and John Newman's strong, raw voice: *'Know I've done wrong, left your heart torn.'* I smile. It is one of my favorite songs. He is screaming in that totally cool way: *'IIIIIIII need to know now, know now, will you love me again?'* I look down at the bouquet in my hand. Bring it to my nose and inhale the faint scent deeply.

'Congratulations, Lana,' I whisper sadly.

No joy shall be equal...

Sixteen

The Yellow Emperor asked: 'How can I know if a woman is close to having an orgasm?'
The simple Girl answered: 'A woman presents five signs and five desires. These are the five signs: First she blushes, now the man can come close to her.'

— Notes from the Bedchamber

I push the button beside the nameplate that reads twenty-five.

'Yes,' a man's voice crackles through.

'It's Julie Sugar. We have an...er...appointment.'

For a few moments there is silence. I interpret it as surprise. We did say Monday? Have I got the date wrong? Is it Monday next? Has he forgotten?

'Take the lift to the top floor.'

The buzzer sounds and I push the heavy door open, into a reception with tall mirrors and flowers. I take the lift to the fifth floor and walk along a blue carpet. I knock on his door and he opens it almost immediately. He is wearing a faded, paint-splattered T-shirt and an extremely old, torn pair of black jeans that hugs his lean hips and strong thighs in a way that makes my eyes want to linger. He is not wearing shoes and his hair is messy in the way David Garrett's gets messy while he is in concert. Silky strands have escaped their tie and hang about his throat.

Sexy.

This man is actually very hot! I feel my throat drying up. Now: if Fat Mary is right about his sexual prowess... My traveling eyes return to his face. In the dim of that heavily curtained room I had not noticed, but, God, what eyes! Fringed with thick lashes and a truly astonishing color. I had thought they were blue. They're not. They are uniquely greenish blue. Like the ocean on a hot day in places like Barbados. They are also totally expressionless. Reserved. Almost cold. Strange. Whatever happened to *that* man with the laughing eyes?

'I was working. I thought you weren't coming,' he says.

'Why did you think I wouldn't come?'

He shrugs. 'People say things, make...er...appointments...' He lets his voice trail off.

I look around the open plan, large, spacious apartment. It is decorated in a modern, non-individualistic but typically masculine way. A sleek sandstone fireplace, black leather sofas, glass coffee table, expensive built-in sound system and oversized plasma screen. Not a plant in sight. There is nothing personal in the flat either. No photographs or scatter cushions that don't match, no collection of anything in glass showcases. But it is situated in the city's prime real estate and must cost a bomb.

'This is a nice place you have.'

'It's not mine. It belongs to Blake. I'm just using it temporarily. The only things that belong to me are my clothes, my CDs, my paints and canvasses, and Smith.'

'Well, it's nice anyway.' I walk to the plate glass wall that stretches from ceiling to floor and look down on London. The view is pleasant. 'Who is Smith?'

'Smith,' he calls and a huge cat, one of those haughty, long-haired, terribly expensive Chinchillas, saunters into the room and goes to rub itself against his legs. He bends down and strokes him. I watch his golden brown hand moving sensuously against the soft fur and I am reminded of Fat Mary's words. He has a slow hand. I walk up to the cat.

'He has the same color eyes as you,' I exclaim.

And he blushes like a girl! It is the first time in my life that I have seen a man go red at something I have said. It makes him appear sweet. To hide, he bends down to pick the cat up.

'In color he is me; in shape he is all you,' he says, finally meeting my eyes. It is my turn to flush. There is something about this man that I respond to on a rather basic level. The cat and I are now at eye level. In his arms it looks like a gray cloud, all soft and fluffy. Smith stares at me with incredibly beautiful, but curiously expressionless eyes.

'Have you had him long?'

'He actually belonged to an ex who decided not to take him back with her when she left for America. She didn't want any reminders of me.'

I look away from the cat towards the stairs that end on a closed door. Vann follows the direction of my eyes.

'That's my work studio. Don't ever go in there.'

My eyes widen. 'Don't go in? Or Bluebeard don't go in?'

'Bluebeard don't go in.' His face is grim. He is serious about this.

'Right. So how do we do this?'

'First you have a shower.'

What? Suddenly I am sitting beside Melissa Brumaster and she is looking at me disdainfully. Melissa Brumaster is a fucking twenty-four carat, first class bitch. 'You smell,' she denounces loudly. Around me girls start giggling. 'Do you never wash?' Her nose is crinkled with disgust. I put my head down and say nothing, filled with the knowledge that she is right. I am fat. I sweat a lot and, like the rest of my family, I don't wash too often. So I stink. That childish taunt has remained in my consciousness. It still hurts like hell today.

'You smell like a perfume counter.'

It is not Melissa Brumaster again. He really doesn't like the smell of perfume! Strange man.

'What will I change into?'

'There's a fresh toweling robe hanging behind the door.'

He turns his thumb in the direction of a door. I march towards it. I hear a chuckle. Bastard. The bathroom is like the rest of the apartment. Sparse, clean and terribly masculine. White on black granite. I strip, leave my neatly folded clothes on a shelf, and enter the shower cubicle. Unlike the leaking showerhead in my home this is the latest in luxury. It is sensationally powerful and I have the best shower I have ever had. In the milky white mist on the glass wall I draw a love heart and an arrow through it. On one side I write Julie and on the other Jack.

I step out, more than a little nervous. I get into the fluffy toweling robe hanging behind the door and feel like a little girl in a large towel. Strangely vulnerable. I look into the mirror. I am not yet used to this new look. And there is something new in my eyes. A glitter that wasn't there before.

It feels as if I am about to enter a fairy tale. And this is the gate where the heroine pauses before taking the first step of the arduous and dangerous journey in her quest to pick the forbidden fruit. The fruit that will wake the sleeping Jack.

My pulse is racing as I go out into the living room. Soft music is playing. Vann appears to have showered too—his hair is damp and he is sitting in a pair of blue jeans and a white T-shirt. The cat is curled up on a cushion beside him. He has a really, really flat stomach. Reminds me of Jack's carved abdomen. Only Jack's abdomen would be pale, like alabaster, and his is a golden brown.

'Are you hungry?'

'I've eaten,' I lie.

'Then you can watch me eat. I'm starving,' he says with a grin, and uncoils himself from the sofa. 'Can I get you something to drink?'

'I'll have a green chartreuse please.'

'A green chartreuse?'

'Yes, have you never heard of it?'

His eyes are amused. 'Yes. Blake's grandmother used to drink it. I didn't think anyone drank it anymore.'

I only said that because I read somewhere that it had been the Queen Mother's favorite drink when she was alive. Other than champagne, and it would have been silly to ask for that, green chartreuse was the most fancy name I could think of. I wanted him to think that I was fancy.

'Here are the choices. Beer or wine, of which I have both white and red.'

'I'll have a glass of white wine please.'

Unsuccessfully hiding a smile, he goes towards the kitchen. I follow him and watch as he opens the fridge.

'I only have dry. Is that OK with you?'

'Great.'

He takes a glass out of a cupboard, fills it half full and, coming over to where I am standing, holds the glass out to me. I take it and he raises his beer bottle to his lips. Swigs it.

'You sure you don't want anything to eat?'

'Positive,' I say and, settling myself on a high swivel chair, observe him expertly grill a steak. I am glad I no longer eat red meat. Meat is full of fat. Still the smell of it sizzling makes my stomach growl. I take a sip of wine. Wine is fattening too. They say it is a hundred calories, but I don't believe them. It must be more. I actually don't like the taste of wine, but I am determined to master my dislike. He cooks fast, efficiently, as if he is used to cooking for himself.

While he cooks we talk. What I do for a living, where he has been—and he appears to have backpacked everywhere. India, Burma, Borneo, Thailand, Africa, South America, Europe. He is only twenty-five, but appears to have done things, some I could never even imagine. In Peking he went to an opium house that had hardly changed from a hundred years ago. He lay on a hard pillow and a beautiful girl rolled out the tiny balls of narcotics and placed them in his pipe. In Burma he stayed in a run-down hotel infested with giant cockroaches. He tells me he lives in a garret in Paris, but he wouldn't move because he likes his bedroom. It reminds him of the painting of Van Gogh's room in Arles, the one with the bed and the dresser.

When the food is ready—steak, mashed potato and salad—he plates it and carries it in one hand while the other curls around a fork and knife.

'Come to the dining table.'

I sit opposite him. He cuts into the piece of meat. Looks juicy. The smell of butter in the mash potatoes fills my nostrils. My mouth waters. This is crazy. He puts the meat into his mouth. I watch his teeth, all straight and white and perfect. An orthodontist's wet dream.

'You sure you don't want some?'

I press my lips together and shake my head. 'I don't eat red meat.'

This is going to be pure torture. He puts his fork into the mash and lightly lifts some onto it, and holds it next to my lips. I look into his eyes. They are crinkled in the corners. To refuse would be churlish. I open my mouth. The fork slips in, I close my mouth over it. The mash *melts* onto my tongue. It is so good I want to close my eyes to savor it fully. I resist the urge. I can taste the butter and some of the juice from the meat. It is so long since I had mash this rich. I let it rest on my tongue and sigh with sheer pleasure.

He pulls the fork out, but his expression has changed. His eyes are no longer crinkled at the corners. They have darkened. He lowers his lids to shutter them. I wonder why. He eats fast and does not offer to feed me any more of his food. The smell and that one mouthful have opened up my appetite. I wish he would offer me another forkful—there can't be that many calories in a bit of mash—but he doesn't.

'Here, let me wash up,' I say for something to do and slip off the chair.

His hand comes out and catches my wrist. A jolt of electricity goes up my arm. This is the second time this has happened. The first time I thought it was caused by the friction between the layers of organza building up static. Now there is not a slither of organza in sight; we are both in cotton. He lets go of my arm. I fight the urge to rub where he has touched.

'Leave it,' he says, rubs his chin and frowns. He pushes his plate away and reaches for his bottle of beer.

'Aren't you going to finish your food?'

'Smith will,' he says abruptly, and gets up. 'Come on. Let's begin.'

I panic. 'Begin? Don't we have some theory first?'

'Sex is all practice, Sugar,' he drawls.

'I need to get drunk first.'

He turns to look at me. Eyes narrowed.

'I've never had sex sober.'

'Never?'

I shake my head.

And he shakes his head in amazement. 'We must remedy that.'

'At least for this time, the first time,' I plead.

'All right, bring your glass.'

We go into the living room. The late evening light has turned the room red gold. On the horizon the sun is a large ball of red. He sits on one sofa and I take the one adjacent to his. I don't know why I am suddenly so nervous. Maybe it is him. He is so dangerously male. The breadth of him, the way his legs are open wide and claiming all that space.

I take a huge gulp of wine. He says nothing. I glug down another large mouthful. And another. There is another last bit left. I knock that back. He is watching me curiously, as if I am a totally different species from him.

'Need more?'

'No.' I haven't eaten and I am a lightweight when it comes to alcohol. In a few minutes I know I will be wasted. In fact, the effect of the alcohol is already beginning to pour into my veins. Making me light-headed, brave.

'Come over here,' he says.

I stand up and go sit next to him.

'Go on,' he invites. 'Show me what you can do.'

I frown. 'I thought you were going to teach me things. What Yehonala did and all that. You know, seduction techniques?'

'This is our first time. No techniques are necessary. The first time you go to bed with any man, the novelty factor will sail you through. Nothing like the first time.'

Boldly, I put my hand on his thigh. An odd sensation in my stomach. Must be guilt. Oh God! Jack. For a moment there I had completely forgotten him. I pull back instantly. I lick my lips. 'Do you have condoms?'

'Of course.'

I peek up from beneath my lashes. 'I might need more drink,' I say, even though my tongue is already numb with alcohol.

He shakes his head.

'Can we at least have less light?'

Seventeen

'Come on,' he says and, getting up, pulls me up by the hand. I stand tipsily and nearly stumble. He looks at me curiously. I flash a brilliantly bold smile. He takes me to his bedroom and closes the blinds by pushing a button on the wall. The curtains are dark wood and the room is immediately thrown into gloom.

'Dark enough for you?' I hear the sex and heat in his voice.

'I think so.'

'Relax. It's only sex.'

'Do you have a girlfriend?'

The pause is almost imperceptible. 'Quit stalling, Sugar.'

I did not realize that he had moved, but he must have, because his hands are around my waist. He smells clean: shampoo and soap. His breath is warm against my neck. I catch the scent of the beer, the meat, and the mash he has consumed. The faint whiff of beer reminds me of that disastrous time with Keith, his breathless grunts, the wet slop of his spunk sliding off my belly.

'I can't do this,' I whisper, and try to pull away.

'Pretend I'm him,' he says, and I freeze.

In my head I enter into a fairy tale. I need to enter the forbidden garden to get the forbidden fruit. To awaken him from his deep slumber so he can escape the clutches of the wicked queen. I feel his hands untying the belt of the robe. I clutch at the edges of the robe. He pulls them away from my grasping hands. Underneath I am naked.

'Your mouth is saying no, but your body is dying for it, Sugar.' His voice is low and seductive.

Temptation floods into me. My breath becomes erratic. I let go of the material. The robe gapes. I am being turned around to face him. His hands are rough but warm. They span my waist. One hand moves upwards and cups my breast. I close my eyes and pretend I am with Jack, but it is impossible. I know I am with Vann. Vann is too large, too magnetic, too golden, too individual, too exciting for me to pretend he is someone else.

'Jack,' I whisper, as if saying his name will make Vann less and him more.

Vann says nothing, simply brings his mouth down on mine while the hands around my waist firmly pull me in so my breasts are crushed into his torso. Something hard presses into my belly. That's one massive erection you've got there, mate.

He takes my fleshy lower lip between his lips and pulls me closer to him. Helplessly my chin lifts. He lets go and starts to kiss me. His lips are softer than I expected. He kisses me as if he is tasting my lips, gently, thoughtfully, almost experimentally.

He opens my mouth with his lips and... Oh! but Vann. He is wet and hot and velvety.

We kiss. We kiss.

All of a sudden sex with a stranger in a dark room becomes insanely desirable. Fucking irresistible. I am no sex kitten but I feel daring, erotic, different. Inside my body, fiery flares of desire are shooting into my brain.

A vixen with *needs* emerges, fully formed and ravenous for fleshy spoils. She couldn't give two hoots about Jack or my great love for him. All she wants is for this enigmatic stranger to fuck her. Hard. In this vast and anonymous flat she knows she can scream as much as she wants. With this stranger who has witnessed her complete humiliation she doesn't have to pretend to be someone she is not. She can be her ugly self. In this dark there is no one to judge her.

She wraps her arms around that stranger's thick neck and pushes her bare body against the gloriously unfamiliar hard planes of his, and feverishly sucks the tongue that is in her mouth. But he holds himself back; he is teasing her, controlling the pace of their kiss, exciting and enhancing the vixen's anticipation.

So the vixen bites the man's withdrawing lower lip and drags her teeth along it making him gasp with surprise and pleasure. Daringly her hands cup the man's tight buttocks, and pull him towards her. She is very strong and the man groans with the realization.

By now the vixen has got used to the dim and can clearly make out her lover's face. His eyes are full of lust, feral lust.

'You're bad, Sugar.'

The vixen smiles knowingly. He picks her up in one easy movement and takes her to the bed. When he has put her on the bed, he begins to unzip his trousers. The vixen draws the soles of her feet closer to her body and lets her knees fall open. With her body arched and her sex exposed, the wanton vixen leaves and Sugar waits to be ravished.

Without clothes he is indescribable. I mean, it's not like I have never seen men like this, I have, but only in magazines. Never thought one of them would be leaning down, his hands on either side of me and running his tongue from the hollow of my throat down to my breast bone. His mouth closes around my nipple. And he sucks it.

'Oh,' I say, surprised by the unfamiliar sensation, the rush of pure desire. The heat between my legs. And a wanting that I have never felt for any other man, except Jack, obviously.

'You like that?'

'Yes,' I whisper in the dark. I shouldn't just be lying here. I should be doing something back to him. But I don't know what to do with my trembling, aroused body. In fact, I don't have the first clue how to seduce this worldly, rugged stranger who is clearly, clearly very experienced and sophisticated. I watch him with widened eyes.

He carries on suckling. The pleasure is exquisite. I close my eyes and arch into his mouth. Suddenly my eyes fly open with shock. He bit me! The pain flares out. He puts his finger on my lips. 'Shhhh...'

The tip of my breast throbs as he puts his palm flat on my belly. I note the desire to meld my body to the silky smooth hardness of his body, hazily. To feel it brushing against my skin as it moves in and out, in and out. In an alcoholic haze I run my hand down the silky muscles, washboard stomach, down, down, down... Erect, thick, mine. Strange how possessive I feel of this stranger's engorged pillar of meat.

I look into his eyes. It has become darker in the room. Impossible to make out the expression. Only the gleam. Like that of a wolf or some night-foraging animal. My legs become numb with desire. He takes my hand in his and makes me swipe my own sex. Jesus, I am soaking wet.

'Juicy Julie,' he says, his voice two octaves lower.

And suddenly I cannot bear the anticipation anymore, the tension building inside me, the ferocious hunger to just fuck his brains out. I just want the tight wet heat inside me to be filled up. To the fucking hilt. I grasp his fingers and push them as deep as they will go into my wet core. My movements are frenzied. Unlike me. I am never this greedy. I was right: two fingers are not enough. I need this man's meat buried deep inside my womb.

I let my hands reach down for his. Solid and heavy and satiny smooth. I want the release I have never had, the one that comes from a cock rammed deep inside me. I begin to move my hands up and down the shaft. Lubrication, Julie. Lubrication.

The other two had wanted me to suck them. I don't like giving blow jobs.

A) Cocks don't taste good raw.

B) I'm just not good at it.

C) It's not pretty, saliva, semen.

D) I don't enjoy it.

So no thanks. Still, Lana has learnt how to deep throat and... I guess I should at least practice some before I take Jack between my lips. I move my mouth towards his shaft. He wraps one hand over the front of my throat. It stops me cold.

'This one's on me, candy girl,' he whispers in my ear, trailing a finger down my stomach, stopping on my pubic bone.

Suddenly the bed shifts. Digging his elbow into the mattress he cups my buttocks in his hands and using his thumbs pries open my inner thighs as he lifts me up to his lips. Very much as if I am a bowl that he intends to drink from. He doesn't drink; he sucks me out. As a schoolboy sucks a toffee. Greedily, with great relish, using his whole mouth, determined to draw out all its flavor and swallow every last bit.

And me, I just moan, squirm and bleat like some dumb animal.

I also cry out whenever he jams his tongue into me. My voice seems foreign to me, as if it belongs to a stranger. He goes from the clit to the hole and back again to the clit over and over until my eyes open to something good and beautiful. I thought the orgasm would never stop. It just went on forever. And when the crown of my head is pushed deep into the pillow and my body is done arching and twisting, he buries his fingers inside and begins to stroke and massage the muscles he finds deep inside me, until they ripple uncontrollably in response and I am tingling all over. It is only then that I realize it is the beginning of another climax. One that I had not rushed towards, one that began in a different place inside my body.

'That's twice,' he says.

My legs are jelly. I'll have to send a thank you note to Fat Mary.

'Open all the way for me,' he says and I hear the tear of the foil wrap. More? Now? Yes, baby.

Seconds later he pushes his cock inside me, but so slowly I want to scream. Fucking millimeter by millimeter. And when he reaches the end, he grinds himself against me and I swear, I scream. And if I didn't my clit does. And just as I think I might be reaching the edge and falling over again he withdraws himself. Slowly, but surely all the millimeters go. And like the tide he comes back in. It goes on following a coded rhythm until I am a boneless, mindless mass of nerve endings and desperate flesh.

The technique is sensational and terrifying. Now I know I am nothing like what I thought. I secretly thought I was borderline frigid. I thought sex with all its smells and emissions was disgusting. What those three guys did to me shouldn't even be called sex. This is a whole different league. His tongue, velvety on the surface and shantung silk underneath, finds its way into my mouth.

I suck it.

Hard.

Skewered by his thick shaft, I move in unison with him, encouraging the sawing of his cock against my clit. An erotic tango. Ah, the sensations. I feel myself building again. My spirit is pressed up against his. We are connected at an indefinable level. We have become one four-legged animal.

I know it is coming, but I am unprepared for the ferocity of the rupture that rips right though me. So explosive that my entire body shudders and vibrates with it and my insides feel like they have melted and are sloshing around hotly inside me.

But he does not stop or allow me time to recover, he carries on pumping into my molten core. His movements so rapid and urgent that they quickly become mine too. This isn't lovemaking anymore. This is pure fucking. And the rest of the world can go to hell.

Then he does something to me I never would have thought I could respond to. He brings his mouth very close to my ear and whispers a one word erotic appeal: come.

And, fuck me, as if I am some sort of push button doll that he owns or as if I really am part of a four-legged animal, I do: groaning, twisting, my hips spasming and carried along on a rush of delirious pleasure. Somewhere on the periphery of my consciousness I feel him jerk and explode inside me. When the world drops back around me he is on his elbows looking at me. I stare at him. Wow! I didn't know it could be like that. If I felt that with this stranger, that I am not even sure I like yet, what am I going to feel when I do it with Jack?

His eyes seem dark in the dimness. He is still firm inside me. I don't move. Whatever is between us is gossamer thin. Even a breath expelled too hard would break it. We have exchanged fluids and essences, we have touched spirits, but there will be no wedding cake, no marquee full of flowers, no champagne toasts, no guests for us. For ours is only a brief interlude, fleeting like the sound of children's laughter as you pass a neighbor's garden. Then wasteland. The thought is strangely bitter.

'I love Jack.'

My voice comes out loud. A shockingly cruel slap. He stills. It is too dark to see the expression on his face. He eases out of me and flips onto his back beside me.

'Are you thirsty?' His voice is even. We could have been polite strangers on a train. *Is this seat taken?*

'Yes.'

'I'll go and get some water,' he says and makes a move to sit up.

'Stay, I'll go and get it.'

I pick the toweling robe from the floor, slip into it and pad out of the bedroom. I need to get away from him. I need time to assimilate what he has done to my body. The entire experience has startled me. I stand in the living room and gaze out of the glass wall into the night. There is a growing moon and no stars.

I'll just be cool. It's just sex. He is not important. I can do anything, say anything, and it won't matter. I see now that I made a good decision. He is the perfect teacher. There is much I can learn from him.

I go past the dining table. His plate is still there, but the meat is gone. The cat has come and eaten it. I look at the mash. Cold, hard mash. I hesitate. Think of the butter, the calories. The cat has probably licked it. I walk away. I pause, then turn back. With my fingers I scoop up the uneaten mash and stuff it into my mouth. I don't taste it. I just swallow the horrid lump.

I suck my fingers and look at the plate. Now he will know I ate his leftovers. I scrape the remaining food into the bin, rinse the plate and put it into the dishwasher. Then I fill a glass with water and leave the kitchen quickly. Away from the scene of my crime. The cat is sitting on its cushion watching me with eerily bright eyes.

'Thank God you can't talk,' I tell it.

I feel the cold mash in my stomach and feel guilty. I'll be good tomorrow.

Eighteen

When I get back he has lit one of the bedside lamps and is lying propped up against the pillows.

I sit on the bed and hold the glass of water out to him. Strangely there is no awkwardness.

'Thanks.'

I watch him drink it. He seems beautiful in this soft light. I let my eyes slide away and look around the room. In front of the bed is a metal pole. Surprised, I turn back to him. 'Is that a lap dancer's pole?'

'Yup. This apartment was rented out to a big gun in the City. And when he left, the pole was left behind.'

'Surely tenants have to leave the place as they find it?'

He shrugs one bare shoulder carelessly.

I swing my legs up on the bed and lean back against the headrest. 'City boys and their drugs and their sluts and prostitutes. What parties he must have had here.'

'Pole dancers are not prostitutes. I've known a few with hearts of gold.'

149

'Oh!' A stab of jealousy. Where on earth did that come from?

'Besides,' he adds, 'the best lap dancers are artistes who turn their bodies into canvasses, works of art. You should try it some time. It's a great turn-on for a man.'

I gaze at him. 'You think I should learn to pole dance?'

'Why not? Jack might love it?'

'And you think my body is good enough for it.'

'The best pole dancers are voluptuous women, but you'll do.'

'Do you think Lana is beautiful?'

He frowns. 'Lana? As in Blake's wife?'

'Mmnn.'

'Yes, very, but a bit too thin for my taste.'

'Is she thinner than me?'

'No, you're thinner.'

'Really?' I feel a warm glow in my stomach. 'I am thinner than her?'

'First time I saw you I wanted to feed you.'

I look at him curiously. 'Why do you like big girls then?'

'They seem more sensuous to me. Their spirit is often more generous.'

The next question seems obvious. 'So why are you sleeping with me then?' His answer is not so obvious.

'Stand up and take your robe off,' he says very softly and there is an underlying steel in his voice.

'No.' My answer is instant and very definite.

'It is my wish that you are naked, whenever I wish it.' He looks at me steadily. Again I am reminded of a hunter. Implacable. He is hunting me without moving a muscle. I want to say no, but that look in his eye. It tells me if I take my robe off there might be more pleasure to come. I have been awakened from a long sexless sleep and now I want more.

I stand and drop the robe, but I am unable to withstand his searing gaze. My hands instinctively go to my breasts and the triangle of hair between my legs in a vain attempt to shield them. He crawls forward on the bed and, standing on his knees, takes away and holds my wrists at the sides of my body.

'Never cover yourself like that again. You were born to be naked.'

He lets my wrists go and sits back on his heels, as proud and naked as the day he was born, and gazes at my body while I struggle not to cover myself.

'Ah, that is lovely,' he whispers finally, and, moving forward, takes a stiff nipple in his mouth.

I gasp.

He sucks.

I tremble. I moan.

He buries his face between my breasts. His lashes sweep darkly against his cheek.

'How can you give pleasure to anyone if you are unhappy in your own body?' His voice is tender now.

I bite my lower lip. He has awakened a strong desire in me. The breast that has been sucked is tingling. As if he has heard my desire, he slips his finger between my legs, and I sigh and part my legs. He takes his hand away and retreats to his haunches.

'Clasp your hands behind your head.'

I obey and find the position has arched my back, thrust my breasts forward, made me feel vulnerable, and in some subtle way increased my nakedness. My whole body flames with desire and shame for my position. He does nothing, just continues staring at me while the slit between my legs begins to swell and feel so very hot. Very naked and helpless, I stand in his gaze.

'You have the most beautiful breasts imaginable. Firm and plump and pink-tipped and so perfectly round they look fake.'

This I know to be true. My breasts are my best assets. They are exactly as he described: pink-tipped, plump and round and without any sag at all. He puts a hand out and curves it around one breast and massages it gently. I shudder helplessly.

'I must have you again.'

He reaches into the dark blonde, damp curls and inserts two fingers into my aching folds. With those fingers impaled in me, he draws me towards him. I gasp. The hand inside me is exquisite, the thought of being pulled by my pussy filthy and erotic. He licks the inside of my thigh. My knees shake.

It happens fast. The other hand wraps around my waist and I am lifted off the ground and placed on the bed. He parts my legs and, gathering the liquids he finds, works my clit, round and round. My hips rise off the bed, my head presses into the mattress, my spine arches.

'Will you totally surrender to me?'

'Yes, yes.'

He smiles. An odd smile. Then he covers my mouth with his hand. Over his hand my eyes open in terror and my body prepares to fight back, but there is nothing to fear, but fear.

'Let's not wake the neighbors,' he says, jams his thumb into me and carries on playing with my clit. But in a special way, as if he is following a set program. Twice my body buckles and tries to find release but at that precise moment he suddenly stops. The frustration builds.

My whimpers are muffled.

Again he looks at the distress in my half-covered face and smiles and carries on playing with my sex even as hot liquid leaks out of it and soaks the sheet underneath. Against my thigh I feel the hard length of him. I begin to twist from side to side, my hands curled into useless fists. My eyes beg him to enter me, finish the job.

Let me have my release.

He shakes his head, bends his head and licks my nipple.

'Let me come,' I sob deliriously under his hand. My whole body is afire.

'Wait,' he says.

153

And works me again, and again—start stop, start stop, God knows how long—until my body is shuddering violently. The spasms coming from deep inside me are so violent that I am shocked and fearful of them. I look at him with frightened eyes. What is he doing to my body?

'Wait,' he whispers. 'This is the real sexual energy that human beings have. This is the thing that ancients use for sex magick. Nothing to fear. It is coming from the base of your spine.'

And indeed the spasms are so powerful that my body is being rocked and lifted cleanly off the bed. And then suddenly it is no longer possible for him to hold me back. I come screaming uncontrollably, awfully, under his hand. The pleasure is indescribable. The release is so great I take great gulps of air. Tears are streaming down my face. My sex is throbbing and what feels like waves or vibrations are expanding out of it. I don't feel tired and wasted, but exhilarated. As if I have taken a really good ecstasy tablet. I look at him through my tears, my shock.

'Wow!'

He smiles. 'That is what Yehonala did.'

'What about you?' I ask, and even my voice sounds different.

'Without selflessness even the best technique is useless.'

He leans forward and kisses the hairy pelt between my legs and withdraws his thumb out of me. And I, I immediately crave it back inside me.

'Are you staying the night?'

God, I actually want to stay. To carry on. This kind of pleasure is explosive, it is addictive. 'I have to go home. Got work in the morning.'

'I'll drive you,' he says evenly, and, moving off me, begins to dress.

The way he switches off immediately makes me feel insecure. I quickly pick up the robe on the floor and wrap it around myself. 'I'll just go change in the other room.'

'OK. Meet me in the living room.'

I look at myself in the mirror and think of Jack and feel guilty. While I was in Vann's bed I had never spared a single thought for him. I dress quickly. When I get back to the living room Vann is already waiting for me.

In the lift I sneak a look at him and find him leaning against the chrome railing watching me. He raises his eyebrows. I think of his thumb jammed like a plug inside me and flush. Quickly I avert my eyes to the lighted numbers. I hate lifts. The doors open and I dash out.

'This way,' he says outside and points to a brand new Jaguar CX Four-by-Four. He opens my door and waits courteously as I climb in.

'Blake's?'

'Of course.'

'It's nice. He's really good to his friends, isn't he?'

'Blake doesn't do friends. There is no one he can trust.'

'But he trusts you.'

'Only because we grew up together. Are you hungry?'

I'm starving. 'Nope.'

'Then I hope you won't mind if I drop by and get a takeaway Chicken Shwarma.'

'Not at all.'

Except for giving him my address, we don't speak much until we get to Beauchamp Place. He parks and turns towards me. 'You sure you don't want anything?'

'I'm sure.'

'OK, won't be a minute.'

I watch him cross the road, his stride long and prowling, and go into a restaurant called Maroush. In less than five minutes he is making his way back to me, two cylindrical white packages in his hand. He gets into the car and opens one package. Is he planning to eat it here in the car, in front of me?

He is. He untwists the top of white greaseproof paper and, tearing it off, reveals the pitta bread filled and rolled with chicken kebab inside. The smell. Oh sweet Jesus. The smell of garlic sauce when you have missed dinner and had a bucket load of sex. He waves it in front of my nose. I know if I ignore the hunger pangs they will go away in a while, but not with the scent of food so close by.

'Just taste it.'

I look at him with an unfriendly expression.

'Go on... It's the best in London,' he cajoles.

One taste. I swallow my saliva, take the package from him and take a small bite. Goodness, gracious me. It is so good I have to stop my eyes from rolling to the back of my head. I try to hand the food back and find him waving it away, and opening the other instead.

'I got you one just in case you changed your mind.'

No further invites are necessary. I bite into the kebab, chew and swallow. And carry on doing so until there is nothing but soggy paper. I gaze at it almost with surprise.

'You were hungry, weren't you?'

Oh shit. I've just eaten a whole kebab at one o'clock in the morning. It's going to become pure fat in my body.

He starts up the engine. There is no traffic on the roads and soon we are outside my block of flats.

'I'll walk you to your door.'

'There's no need. See that door there?' I say, pointing to my door on the third floor. 'That's my home.'

We exchange numbers.

'Wednesday at seven. Don't eat before you come over and bring some clothes and the stuff you need in the morning. Plenty of empty cupboards for you to choose from.'

'OK,' I say and jump out of the car.

He waits until I have run up three flights of stairs. I wave before I enter my home and close the door. Everybody is asleep. I go into the kitchen and fill a glass with water. I salt the water. I drink three glasses. Then I run up to the bathroom and make myself sick. There, all that horrible fatty meat is gone from my body. Tears are streaming down my cheeks, but I feel light and good again.

I flush the toilet, clean my teeth, spray some air freshener and go to bed.

Nineteen

It is 9.10 when I leave home for work. On the way I see two men putting up a billboard poster with a pair of eyes looking out of punched out gray wallpaper and the caption, 'We're closing in on undeclared income'. The poster is from Her Majesty's Revenue Collection Department. It is designed to put the fear of God into people who are evading or planning to evade tax.

People like me. Who pretend to work sixteen hours a week, but in actuality work many more. Fuck them, I think. They honestly make me so mad. It's bullshit that taxes are used to raise revenue. Imagine putting up a poster like that in such a poor and depressed area, and there are all these giant multinational corporations getting away scot-free with not paying billions in taxes.

As far as I am concerned they are just bullies to come after little people like me. It is not the likes of me that are killing the economy, but them. Think about it. If I revealed the exact number of hours I work, they would tax not only me, but also the small business I work for. My employer would then no longer be able to afford my services and run aground. Besides, they don't need my little contribution at all. They proved that when they suddenly and magically found billions to bail out the big banks with. Income tax is a tax to work. And I'm not fool enough to pay tax to work.

I unlock the door of Sasha's Flowers and disarm the alarm. I switch on the lights and the computer and check if any orders have come in during the night. There are none. I put on my apron, sweep and mop the place. As I am changing the water in the pails of flowers Zipporah comes in.

She stops in the doorway, narrows her eyes. 'What have you done to yourself?' she demands.

'Nothing.'

'You're glowing.'

I flush hard.

'You had sex last night, didn't you?'

'No, I didn't.'

'Yes, you surely did. Look at you, you're as red as a Walker's crisp packet.'

'All right, I did. But I don't want to talk about it.'

'So it's not the boy, then?'

Ziporrah is the only one who kind of knows about the crush I have on Jack.

'No,' I mutter.

'Hon, if a man can make you look this good, you should kick that boy to the curb, and get with the man.'

Let me tell you about Ziporrah. She has all her hair in tiny cornrow braids and the type of hourglass figure you would see in a rap music video, the butt so high and rounded you could eat dinner on top of it. Her mother named her after the wife of Moses. Yeah, I didn't know either, but apparently she was black! On a plaque hanging on the wall in the shop Ziporrah has part of a verse from the Song of Solomon 1:5: "I am black and beautiful."

The thing about Ziporrah is that she is unashamedly black. She doesn't try to straighten her hair, color it, or do anything to 'whiten herself'. She always tells it like it is. In fact, nothing infuriates her more than white people who think they are doing her a favor by using 'the n word' instead of nigger in her presence.

'Cause that just means you have to say the word in your head for them. Black people have a chip the size of Africa on their shoulder because their blood remembers the time they were sold like oxen. But underneath their skin, they're just like you, girl. Only less fucked up.'

I choose the flowers I want to use in my flower arrangement and lay them down on the wooden table in the back room of the shop. I start my arrangement with a pink rose stalk (desire) and follow that with an oleander (caution).

In my head, Vann says, 'Let's not wake the neighbors.'

Twenty

It feels strange to be taking an overnight bag to a man's home. When I think about it, he has practically invited me to move in. When I arrive at Vann's he is already out of his work clothes. I have made a point of not using any perfume.

'It has turned out to be a glorious spring evening, too beautiful to be staying indoors. I thought we could go out to eat.'

'OK.'

'I know a fantastic Indian restaurant.'

Indian food. No way. Not only is it extremely fattening, but it burns all the way up and out. 'Poo on a plate? No thanks,' I say very firmly.

'What?'

'That's what Indian food looks like to me. Diarrhea on rice.'

He looks incredulous. 'You lump all Indian food as poo on a plate?'

'Yeah.'

He shakes his head. 'You need re-education badly, Sugar.'

Nothing I say moves him. He takes me to his friend's restaurant on a side street off Piccadilly Circus and orders half a portion of what seems to me to be almost everything on the menu. And I am *told* I have to taste at least one bite of everything. He does not order any alcohol.

'It dulls the senses,' he says. 'And tonight you are going to have a sensory overload.'

I take a sip of still mineral water. 'So where did you learn all the stuff you did to me the other day?'

'Conversation is not allowed either.'

I smile. I'm game if it ends up the way of the other night.

A beautiful waitress passes by and he doesn't even glance.

I raise my eyebrows. He raises his back. I smile. His smile is polite but mocking.

All kinds of dishes are placed in front of us— chicken marinated in tamarind, fiery pork with kachampuli, succulent lamb in a full-bodied black sesame seed curry, tandoori prawns laden with clarified butter and lime. Silently, I take a bite of the cubes of fried bones in an orangey-red Amritsari sauce. I follow that with fish marinated in yogurt and pungent potatoes in an old ancient Kashmiri recipe.

Sometimes I close my eyes to fully appreciate the foreign flavors. When the tiger prawns marinated in green chilies and mustard paste and cooked inside a green coconut until tender and bursting with flavors causes my eyes to water a glass of hot water is given to me. An old Indian trick. Only hot water will stop the burning. It works. What's left on my tongue is ginger, garlic, lime, red chilies, ajwain, Indian sorrel and a silence pregnant with erotic intent.

'Dessert?'

I shake my head. I've had enough.

'Mango kulfi,' Vann says.

When it comes, he spoons it into my mouth. Our eyes meet, lock. For the first time that night I swallow without tasting.

In the end I have to confess that none of it is poo on a plate.

'Never dismiss an entire culture like that again,' he says.

He has not turned on the light but the illumination from the moon turns him bronze as he pulls his shirt off. I drink in the sight of the powerful arms and shoulders, the broad chest, the taut stomach. Rising to my knees I reach and touch his stomach with my fingertips. His eyes are hooded and burning with desire. My fingers move to the waistband of his jeans. I undo the button and grasp the zip.

And then I lose my nerve and pull my hand back, but he catches the edge of my T-shirt, tugs it over my head and, swiftly and with unnerving expertise unhooks my bra. He unzips my jeans, pushes me back onto the bed and tugs the jeans off by pulling the material at the ankles. He throws them behind him and hooking two fingers on either side of my knickers, pulls them down.

'And that is how it is done,' I whisper throatily.

He chuckles and, turning away from me, crosses the room and opens the door to one of the built-in cupboards. I get on my elbows and watch him curiously. He brings out what looks like a wooden object. It is about nine inches long, thick on one end and pointed on the other. I sit up in alarm.

'You're not going to put that in me, are you?'

He laughs. 'By the time I am finished you're going to be wishing I had.'

'I'm not into kinky things.' My voice is very sharp, although I am disturbed to note that I am actually secretly turned on. 'I'm here purely to learn how to seduce Jack.'

'Very altruistic of you,' he says drily. 'This...instrument...is for a foot massage.'

I lie back down. The mattress depresses and he sits cross-legged before the soles of my feet. 'The first few massages will be painful, but eventually you will come to crave it. In ancient times only the concubine that is chosen to spend the night with the wealthy warlord would be given a foot massage. It made all the girls long to be chosen for the night.'

He grasps my foot by the ankle and, raising it to his lips, kisses the sole. The gesture is incredibly sexual and I feel myself instantly respond. Slowly, he drags the blunt end over my feet. That's not bad. Quite nice actually. I change my mind fast when the sharpened end meets my skin and sharp blots of pain go up my leg. I try to withdraw my leg, but he holds on tight.

'You want to bind the man to you?'

Reluctantly I nod.

'Then you must learn the method. If you cannot bear it yourself, how will you dispense it?'

I bite my lips and agree to go all the way.

'Even if you beg me to stop?'

'Even if.'

But the pain is so horrible I stop squirming and start shouting and finally beg him to stop.

He says nothing. Simply works that torture instrument until finally he stops. Relieved, I take in my first full breath. Then he grasps the other ankle.

But eventually it is over. I am bathed in a film of perspiration, but strangely alive. All my nerve endings are so sensitive that when he takes my tender, throbbing big toe in his mouth and sucks it the pleasure is so intense my back becomes a tightly drawn bow, and I simply don't want it to stop. Ever.

He makes short work of getting out of his jeans and briefs, unrolls a condom on his erection and crawls on top of me.

'How do you feel?'

'Tingly and silky all over, but mostly just relieved.'

He laughs softly. 'That's what l like to see: a damp and glowing but precocious woman.' He bends down and kisses one breast peak. 'Ready?'

'Yes.'

'This one is called the Flying Dragon—you probably know it as the missionary position.' He puts his hands under my knees and lifts them until the soles of my feet are flat on the mattress. That opens my pussy. I raise my thighs, eager for him to plunge into me. He lays the palms of his hands on either side of me.

'Two deep, eight shallow. Enter softly,' he says, and feeds his hard flesh slowly into me until he is buried deep inside. I suck at him with my muscles, trying to pull him even deeper into me. 'Withdraw hard,' he says, and pulls out so suddenly, I yell. He thrusts from the hips, the rhythm relentless.

Two deep, eight shallow, enter softly, withdraw hard. Together we delve deeper and deeper into a place I have never been to, but desperately want to explore. It is dark and throbbing and warm, and wild with ecstasy.

I feel large but gentle hands on my body. I am eased to my knees, brought to my elbows, face down, ass up high. My thighs are parted. 'This position is called the Tiger's Walk. Not every woman can enjoy this—the thrusts are deep.'

And indeed they are—the first plunge is so deep it feels as though he will come out of my throat. But I like it. I love the feeling of being so filled up, so stretched. I can feel his dick wading thickly through my juices. Again and again he hammers into me, with a definite but different rhythm from the last position. Five short, eight deep. When my own syrupy liquids start running down my thighs, he stops and turns me over.

He lifts my legs until my knees touch my breasts and my lower back and buttocks are raised in the air. He presses down hard, almost ferociously on my body, and enters me violently. I thought his shaft had entered me deeply before but with this position he reaches my deepest core. I gasp with shock, and before I know it my entire body is contracting with long spasms, the kind that I imagine women in labor have to endure. I give in to it, and a wave takes me over a crest and beyond. I am flying alone, even with him there, always alone. But it is beautiful where I go.

When the eruptions settle down, I find him looking down at me.

'You're sweet.'

'You never came,' I accuse.

'I have a fantasy, Sugar. Ever since I saw you I wanted to come in your mouth.'

'I'm not sure I'm all that good at giving head.'

'There's no secret to a good blow job. Simply suck it as if you want to suck it dry. Pump it to death.'

He removes the condom. I get between his legs and fit my lips around his rock-hard cock. Above me he sighs. I take his advice and suck like my life depends on it. I look up at him and he is watching me, his eyes glazed and unreadable. His hands are on either side of my head. As I watch him his expression changes into a snarl, his head goes back and he spurts into my mouth.

It never crosses my mind to move my head back or spit out the semen. I swallow. It's only protein. And I like protein. For a moment I am shocked at my own behavior. I am normally so fastidious and yet, after I have swallowed it all, I lick his steaming cock as if it is a lollipop. I lick it until it is clean of every last drop of cum.

'Your mouth is so warm and sweet, I wish I could fall asleep with my cock in your mouth,' he says.

Instantly, I take the semi-hard meat back into my mouth, but he pulls me upwards so his dick slips out with a slapping sound, and brings me up to his face.

'My heart just skipped a beat,' he says.

'That's funny, so did mine.'

We smile at each other. His lips touch my eyelids. It is tender and intimate. I sigh with pleasure. He tightens his hold on my arm and I tremble. A craving stirs in my veins. *This man is mine*. What the hell is that thought all about? It brings me up short. It is like a bucket of cold water in my face. *Jack is mine.* Not him.

He is just teaching me...things. I am going to recreate everything I am doing with him with Jack. And it will be so much better and greater because I love Jack. I pull away from him, disengage my body from his, and plonk myself on the pillow next to him.

'If Yehonala was a virgin, who taught her?' My voice sounds cool.

'In Yehonala's time sex was seen as an art and the climax of human emotions. To achieve the right sexual alchemy meant years of dedication, application and energy. Before she could enter the bedchamber and lie on the red silk sheets of the Emperor, she knew she had to become master of her craft.'

'The craft of sex.'

'Yes. There were women in Yehonala's time who could take a pistachio nut and an egg yolk into their mouth, and spit out chewed nut and a whole yolk. Today stone eggs are used as a cheap sexual trick. In her time they were placed inside the body and used as a point of resistance against which the vaginal and pelvic floor muscles could be strengthened and trained in conjunction with a series of complicated exercises. An adept could massage a man's penis in opposing directions. Yehonala would have been taught other closely guarded secrets that are only revealed to the Emperor's concubines and she would have practiced on skillfully crafted, bronze prostheses of male organs.'

'Where did you learn all this stuff?'

There is a pause. 'Mostly in India and China. And some things in a monastery in Tibet. I've got some books I've asked a friend to send over. They'll be here in the next couple of days. You can study them, if you want.'

'Thanks.'

There is something else I want from him. 'So: your family worked for Blake's?'

Instantly I sense it, the imperceptible stiffening. The pitch of his voice shifts to non-committal and elusive. 'Yes.'

'And you all grew up together?'

'Mmnnn.'

I turn on my side and face him. 'What was life like?'

He sighs. 'Why do you want to know?'

'Why wouldn't I want to know about a world peopled by royalty, tycoons, celebrities, high society parties and fancy lives?'

He looks at me with a despairing expression. 'You watch the Kardashians, don't you?'

'Of course. The best show on TV ever. Now, tell me about the Barringtons and don't leave anything important out,' I demand.

'It was a jewel-encrusted cage,' he says abruptly.

'Why do you say that?'

'Because it was. Marcus, Blake and Quinn lived in magnificent palaces stuffed with the furniture of Louis XV, the paneling of Bourbon kings, priceless paintings, Gobelin tapestries, and ate from Sèvres porcelain set on golden server plates stamped with the family crest. More than thirty people worked in the house as butler, head housekeeper, chef, footmen, maids, nurses, chauffeurs and at least another sixty were employed on the farm, stable and gardens.

'The children ate sitting straight-backed, eyes ahead and mostly silent with footmen in livery and spotlessly white gloves standing behind their chairs. The food was of the highest quality and prepared by a renowned French chef. Thousands was spent on fish alone, but their menu never varied. Mondays was fish, Tuesday was fowl, Wednesday was meat, Thursday was back to fish and so forth. Everything was controlled, from when they awakened to when they went to bed, what they ate, how they dressed, what they did. Every hour had to be accounted for. It was a very strict upbringing.

'All the Fabergé eggs, all the gilt and the gold did not make life less stiflingly immaculate or incessantly boring. The simple fact was their childhood was one of physical luxury combined with personal neglect. It was designed to make one emotionally ill, but unable to express the trauma as nobody would understand. Blake once told me his only friends were his horses.'

I stare at him with surprise. 'Why? Did they have no friends then?'

'Very few, and even those they met only occasionally. Eventually they understood they were different from everybody else. It is very difficult to trust anyone when you know that almost every person that befriends you is motivated by self-enrichment.'

I immediately think of that day when Lana told Blake her father wanted money, and there had been not even the least trace of surprise in him. In fact, he had expected it. Still, I wanted to hear about their parties.

'Did they not have fantastic lawn parties full of beautifully dressed people then?'

'Of course. The Barringtons, like all the other families, tried to outdo each other in the lavishness of their parties. I remember gardeners used to carry cherry trees around the dining table so guests could pick the fruit themselves.'

This is more like it. 'Who were the guests?'

'It was a heady mix of the rich and the rarefied, artist and royalty, beauty and brains, Indian maharajas and smarmy politicians. They came to sample every imaginable pleasure. It was an amazing sight, people dressed in all their jewels and grandest most opulent dresses streaming up the stairs from the ballroom. But what I remember most is how dark and gloomy it always was, after all the glamorous people were gone and the chandeliers had been switched off. It was a suffocating existence. A place to escape.'

Twenty-one

Thursday, after I leave Vann's flat, turns out to be the most boring day of my life. From the moment my alarm jerks me from sleep I go through the entire day like a zombie and I am almost joyfully thankful when my head hits the pillow—the day is over. When I wake up on Friday it is with sheer excitement. I have so much adrenalin rushing in my veins I run to work, rush through my chores, leave work early, bathe, dress, and am out of my flat like a bat out of hell.

On the platform, I glance impatiently at the board showing that a train will arrive in four minutes. On the train my toe taps. Out of the Tube station, a girl beggar pleads for loose change. I hurriedly slip my hand into my front jeans pocket, grasp a few coins and, without looking at what I am giving away, drop them into the jacket she has spread on the ground in front of her.

When I arrive at the entrance to his building my hands shake as I look for the keys he gave me Thursday morning. I let myself into his flat, close the door, and stand for a moment at the threshold.

The entire place is flooded with evening sun, and silent. There is not even Smith around. Then I hear a noise from upstairs. I look up. The door is shut. He is working. My instructions are simple. If you come in and I am working, don't disturb. *Never* come upstairs.

Without Vann's presence, the scrupulously clean flat is still and strange. I go into the living room and find a book and a note. The book is called *Notes From the Bedchamber*. I pick the note up.

It arrived. See you soon. x

I smile at the little kiss. I take the book, curl up on the big black leather sofa and open it. Soon I am giggling aloud. It is full of flowers descriptions and sex positions. A penis is a jade stalk, a pussy is described as a jade portal, jade chamber, red pearl, but the one that gets me really giggling is when it is referred to as a fragrant mouse.

I hear the upstairs door open and instead of looking up I carry on reading. Soon master and cat are standing next to me. I don't look up. The sofa beside me shifts. A man's hand comes into my vision. He starts unbuttoning my blouse.

'Do you want to put your jade stalk into my fragrant mouse?' I ask, barely able to keep the laughter out of my voice.

'Desperately,' he says and we both laugh.

'Do you want to go out?'

I shake my head. The truth is, ever since I discovered sex, all I want to do is have sex all the time. Even right now with two buttons undone it feels like unfinished business.

'OK, I'll go get in the shower and you can start preparing some food.'

'I can't cook.'

His eyebrows rise. 'Right. What do you plan to feed Jack when he comes home from work?'

I frown. I never thought about that. In my dreams we never did anything as mundane as cooking or eating.

'I'll have my shower and we'll cook something together. It's time you learned.'

I smile. 'Good thinking, Batman.'

He nods, pushes himself off the sofa and leaves in the direction of the bedroom. Smith fixes his eyes on me and yawns from the sofa opposite. I button my blouse and turn my eyes back to reading about mounting turtles, mating cicadas and jumping monkeys.

We cook chicken with rice. The rice is a boil in the bag variety so that will be really easy for me to replicate, but the chicken is another matter. It is some kind of Moroccan recipe with a whole load of ingredients. But I realize that cooking is actually fun. Vann is great company and it is a laugh.

When the food is nearly ready we lay the table and Vann lights some candles. The food is delicious.

'Have you sold lots of paintings?'

'I've never sold a painting.'

'Not a single one?'

He shakes his head. 'No.'

I frown. 'Well, don't you think you should start thinking about doing something else if nobody wants to buy your paintings?'

'I've never tried to sell my paintings.'

'Why?'

'I've destroyed everything I've ever painted.'

I stare at him. 'Why?'

'Wasn't good enough.' His voice is light, but I feel the intensity behind his words. I can't connect.

I spear a piece of chicken and put it into my mouth. 'What is it you are aiming for?'

He puts down his fork. 'I want to make art that means something.'

I look at him blankly.

'Do you know anything about art?'

I shake my head. 'My knowledge of art starts and ends with recognition of the Mona Lisa as one of the greatest paintings.'

'The destruction of art began in 1917 when an ignorant Dadaist, Marcel Duchamp, re-orientated a urinal ninety degrees from its normal position and called it art. It was actually a challenge from an anti-art advocate. Art, he was saying, is meant to be pissed on, but the fools who act as gatekeepers in the art world turned around and embraced the urinal, saw beauty where there should have been none.'

My eyebrows rise. 'Really? A urinal was considered art?'

'With that one move he turned the experience of art away from a quest for beauty into a sense of distaste. The viewer is presented with something ugly, tasteless, depressing and empty of any technical skill, and asked to admire it. If he cannot then he must be an intellectual philistine. To make it in the new art world all the artist had to do was can his own excrement, submerge a crucifix in his own urine; saw a calf in half, pickle it in brine, and exhibit it in a glass case; stud a skull with diamonds, or liquidize goldfish in blenders. So modern art became a smirking, degenerate thing whose sole purpose seems to be to trivialize or destroy.

'But the truth is real beauty is rare, and producing it even harder. Far from being an old-fashioned idea, beauty has the ability to tantalize and crush. Humans have an intense response to beauty. In all aspects of life we worship it: people, fashion, photography, homes, nature, films. We are even obsessed. My aim is simple. I want to create dangerous beauty.'

I stare at him, his passion. He seems beautiful beyond what I thought. At that moment I admire him. Am I like that with flowers? Maybe. No. Definitely not. I love flowers, but I could easily live without them. The search for the perfect arrangement does not consume me. I have quite happily sent out flower arrangements that were not the best that I could do. I have never destroyed even a mediocre arrangement. Ziporrah would kill me if I did. He, on the other hand, is committed to producing something great, and until he does he will not rest.

'You really love your art, don't you?'

'Art is the only thing that has ever taken me away from the bullshit. They can take away all my possessions, but they can never take away my art.'

'So how do you make money to live then?'

'I had a small amount of money left to me. Blake manages it for me.' And then he closes over, and I wish I had not asked him about money. He was beautiful when he was talking about art.

After dinner we put the dishes in the dishwasher and Vann feeds Smith. Afterwards he turns to me. 'Ready to be ravished?'

I grin. 'Since I walked through the door.'

He takes my hand and starts running to the bedroom with me following and laughing. In the bedroom he stops. 'I want a striptease.'

I start unbuttoning my top and then I have to laugh. This is just not me.

'When you take your clothes off, have a plan. Don't fuck around.'

'That's easy for you to say, you're not doing it.'

'Do you want me to?'

I jump on the bed and lie with my hands linked behind my head. 'Ladies and gentlemen, Vann Wolfe will be taking his clothes off now.'

Looking into my eyes he grasps the edges of his T-shirt and pulls it over his head, his head flowing back gracefully, challengingly. I whistle. Ignoring me he tugs his boots and tosses them behind him.

I raise an eyebrow to distract him, but he smiles and nods as if to say, I know your game.

He rolls his socks, one at a time, down, and eases them off. Then he points his toes away from me, twists his torso and unbuckles his brown leather belt. Pulls it through the loops and lets it dangle from one finger. By now you'd think I'd be holding my belly, splitting my sides from laughing, but no. I am in thrall.

Already I can feel his pulse as he sinks his cock deep into me.

He grasps the button next. The zip peels away. A white bulge. The faded jeans slide down, down, down. My pussy starts to quietly sob. He turns to face me. Doesn't pose or anything. Just stands there, panther-like, in his jockeys. I try to look for imperfections. Is he too broad? No. His hips too narrow? Nope. Hair too long? Possibly. But in the end any imperfections only make for his perfection and I am throbbing with excitement. Unsustainable psychedelic jolts are shooting through my body, paralyzing me. I know how this unfolds. It unfolds in a tangle of limbs with me being speared right between the legs. But it's the waiting that's the killer.

'What are you waiting for? Take it off.' My voice sounds like a sleep time purr.

He vaults onto the bed suddenly, startling me. I squeal inelegantly.

He leans back against the pillow, his hands behind his neck. 'Some things have to be earned.'

A rush of pure lust floods me. The ripples keep on happening. 'No kidding,' I say and peel his underwear off.

His eyes flare with excitement. Like a parrot that is offered a peanut. I lick his cock like it is a melting ice cream, upwards. His cock is thick, salty, satin on my tongue. I like that. A calorie-free treat. That's a mental tattoo. A voice in my head. Keep it light and sexy, Sugar. I wrap my lips over it and swirl my tongue around it.

'I wish I could be your angel.'

That's heavy stuff. 'Why?'

'Make you see.'

'See what?'

'Never mind. We're not on the same page.'

That's fine then. I don't want to talk. There is a storm in my pussy trying to find its way home.

Then I go back to mindlessly sucking thick, salty satin. When he flips me over and does his thing, and the release comes, it is insanity in a bucket.

Ciao, everybody.

Twenty-two

I dream of painting and then I paint my dream.
—Vincent Van Gogh

When the urge hits you, it's hard to resist. That afternoon on the way to Vann's it hits me. I speed-walk to Tesco, grabbing two packets of crisps from the newsagents on the way, because I can't wait that long to shove something down my gullet. I whizz around the supermarket almost in a panic, piling my basket with *anything* at all that takes my eye. I have everything I fancy. And I mean everything.

The woman at the checkout, an old dear, smiles. 'Having a party?'

Grasping my plastic bag, I hurry as fast as I can to Vann's flat. I get in and it is quiet. He is working upstairs. I know he will not come out for hours yet. I sit at the dining room table and, opening my stash, I begin to gorge. Quickly, as if I am in a race. Stuffing my mouth, hardly chewing, swallowing. Savoury followed by sweet, sweet followed by savoury, savoury followed by sweet. I race through the food. Racing. Racing. When I am almost full I relax. I eye the food left over on the table. There is still more space inside me. I indulge again. Until I am so stuffed I can hardly breathe. I relax. The panic has gone...

Instead I feel a sick smugness, a delicious comfort that I can actually get away with eating a whole pack of biscuits, half a chocolate fudge cake, an entire box of cream cakes, half a tub of ice cream, five packets of crisps, half a cold pizza and cheese macaroni. I can have the last laugh.

I go to the tap and drink as much water as I can. Then I go to the bathroom, hang my head over the toilet bowl and reverse all that damage. I am sitting on the floor, tears in my eyes, the disgusting smell of my own vomit rising around me, when the door opens and Vann is standing there. For a while he says nothing, simply looks at me.

In my head I hear a hiss, like the hiss of limestone caves. For those moments I am terrified that I will see disgust and rejection in his face. I have excuses up my sleeves. I have had them for a long time. Only I haven't ever had to use them before. I open my mouth. He comes forward, lightning quick, two strides. He crouches beside me and put his fingers on my lips.

'I saw the packets. It's all right.'

And I slump against the wall. Relieved that no lies are necessary. Relieved that another human being knows. Relieved that it is him and not Jack.

With him it doesn't matter. With him I can be myself. Show my true face. Even the ugly one. He accepts me just as I am. Everything that I am. There is no need to pretend or hide.

'I was once very fat,' I whisper.

'The other kids were cruel?'

'Vicious.'

'Hmnnnn...'

'I'm afraid the damage is invisible but extensive.'

'Hmnnnn...'

'I don't do it all the time. I'm not bulimic or anything.'

'I know. Afternoons and evenings are the hardest, huh?'

'Yeah.'

'It's when your blood sugar dips lowest.'

'I'm sorry.'

'You've nothing to be sorry for, Sugar.' He stands up, flushes the toilet, takes a face towel from the rail, and goes to the sink. I watch him open the mixed tap, and wait with his finger in the water stream, and only when it is warm does he wet the edge of the towel. He comes towards me, gets on his haunches and gently wipes my face.

I feel so confused. Someone once told me, it is in the little things that people reveal their true nature. Anyone can make the grand gesture, light up the sky once with a banner that says, 'I love you,' but it is the man who gives you the ripest cherry in the bowl that you want. That thing he had done with the water, waiting for it to warm up, that was beautiful.

A little voice in my head: he'll make a great husband to some lucky girl. Another thought comes after that, but that thought I don't allow to sprout. I love Jack. Jack is my dream. I've loved Jack all my life and I *will* marry Jack. Not for anything in the world will I give my Jack up.

He brushes the hair from my face. 'Is there something else you need to do to end this...ritual?'

'Yeah, I need to clean my teeth. Stomach acid wreaks havoc with your teeth.'

He stands and holds his hands out to me. I take them and he hoists me up. I move towards the sink and he sits on the edge of the bath while I clean my teeth. I spit and meet his eyes in the mirror.

'You're beautiful, Sugar. Every inch of you. Don't let anybody tell you differently. I came down to ask you to come up. I want to paint you.'

'You want me to come up into your studio?'

He smiles. 'But you can't look at any of the canvasses. That's the deal.'

'I won't look. But one day you'll show me, right?'

'Maybe. I'm working on something that's looking good.' And his eyes shine.

He makes me drink a large glass of water first, then we go up the stairs together. He opens the door and we are standing in a room that is mostly made of glass. Even half the ceiling is glass. Natural light is pouring in. I turn to look at him.

'It is the most perfect studio.'

He nods, but he is different here.

'Take off your clothes.'

'What, in this bright light?'

'You were born to be naked, Sugar. There is nothing more beautiful than the naked human body.' His voice is low, compelling. Totally irresistible. I stare into his eyes. 'Especially yours.'

I want to ask why especially mine, but I can't. I feel hypnotized by his gaze. He takes me over to a couch that has had a red sheet thrown over it and strategically placed red cushions.

'You will be desired, cherished and possessed for the very things you are ashamed of,' he tells me.

He sucks my bottom lip until it is gorged with blood and swollen. He stands back to see what he has done and nods with satisfaction. Then he starts to undress me. Slowly, deliberately. As my top comes off, he kisses my neck. 'Beautiful,' he murmurs into the hollow of my throat. My bra falls on the floor and he gazes at the pink tips, then back to my eyes. His eyes are alive. His hands work on my jeans. He crouches on the ground and pulls them off.

I look down on his head and have such a strong desire to push his face into my crotch that I have to flex my hands. The knickers come off easily, next the shoes, the little pink pop socks.

Naked as a flower I stand over him.

'Legs apart,' he says and I spread them. He buries his face between my legs and licks at the wet slit. My mouth opens.

The artist looks up at my face, his mouth glistening with the oils from my sex. 'There, that expression, that's what I want.'

He lays me on the couch. Arms flung out on the cushions, legs open and bent at the knee. It is the most sexually arousing thing to lie there with my legs open, and have him stand over me and avidly watch my wet, open pussy. My arousal did not come from any expectation of what could take place, but from the act of exposing myself.

'Keep that expression,' he says and moves away to paint.

I don't need to ask if the picture will be pornographic. I know it won't. I know his art is the most important thing to him. For an hour neither of us speaks. Then he does his brushes in turpentine, cleans them on a rag, puts cling film over his palette and comes to me.

He covers my throbbing pussy with his whole hand. 'I am going to eat you until you scream.' Then puts his mouth where his hand has been and sucks me so hard I gasp.

He looks at me. 'Want me to stop?'

I don't speak. I grab him by the hair with both hands and pull him towards my cunt. He licks and sucks every inch, lapping it all up like a cat. He comes up and, with the taste of me still on his tongue, bites my mouth. Devouring me like a mad man or a crazed animal. There is none of the control of our 'lessons'.

The sex is violent. He slams into me. It is almost as if this is a punishment or his inability to control a reckless desire for me. I burn bright as lava moves through my bloodstream. It feels as if every orifice and pore on my body is open and breathing him in.

He goes back to my sex and sucks and bites me there until I am raw and still I have the sensation that he is not able to get enough. Minutes that feel like hours pass. I come in a rush and as soon as I have, he withdraws out of me and comes on my stomach. His seed is like thick hot drops of rain. Unlike the slide of cold gunk on my belly when I had let that boy humiliate me with his emissions.

He leans on his elbow and watches his handiwork. The tousled hair, the swollen red lips between my open legs, the thoroughly fucked look in my half-hooded glazed eyes and my slack mouth. He trails his fingers up my cheek.

'I'm sleeping with my muse,' he says gently.

Still floating, I smile mistily.

It is dark when we go downstairs. He goes to have his shower and I stand in the living room in a robe looking out of the glass walls. It is a clear night and all the stars are out.

'What are you doing?' he whispers in my hair.

'Watching the stars.'

'You are the only woman I have known who appreciates the stars.'

'It always surprises me that stars are enormous suns. They look so cold,' I say softly. 'Often I open my curtains and look out at them. I know that thousands of miles away these are the same stars that are looking down on Jack, and that makes me feel closer to him. Through them we are connected. And I go to sleep peaceful in my heart.'

'Have you read *The Little Prince*?'

It embarrasses me that I know so little compared to him. 'No.'

'*And at night you will look up at the stars...and in one of the stars I shall be living. I have to go to the stars. And one day, when you look at the stars, you will remember me.*'

'What does it mean?' I breathe. I know it is profound, but my brain is unable to process it.

His shallow breathing is in my ear, his scent, the warmth of his hard body pressed against mine...all mingled together to send a warm glow of arousal to spread in the pit of my belly. But I do, I really do want to know what he means about the stars. He takes a lock of my hair and winds it slowly in his finger.

And kisses me.

The desire for the secret knowledge about the stars recedes, but does not go away. I know it is important. It contains a hidden message. A clue.

A voice louder than all the others says: 'You are here to learn how to seduce Jack.'

Jack! Of course, Jack. My true love.

Twenty-three

When I enter the apartment the studio door is shut and Smith is nowhere to be seen, so I assume Vann is working. I go straight into the shower and wash off the smells of the Underground, the sweat and the despair of the people in it.

Vann has left a note taped to a CD for me.

I first heard this played in an open-air restaurant in Thailand. It reminds me of you.

I put the CD in the music system and hit play. The room fills with the pretty sounds of a guitar, a hi-hat and a tambourine.

Sugar, ahhh, honey, honey you are my candy girl...

It is the original 1969 Archies version of 'Sugar, Sugar'. It makes me smile and lifts my heart. I replay it, and nodding my head, dance around goofily. Funny, I have never been this happy in my life.

I decide that I, too, should send him something. I know his favorite poet is William Butler Yeats. So

I Google him and come across the poem 'He wishes for the Cloths of Heaven' I learn the last three lines by heart. I smile to myself. Later when we are lying in bed together I will recite them to him. I will surprise him.

> But I, being poor, have only my dreams;
> I have spread my dreams under your feet;
> Tread softly because you tread on my dreams

It's still too early to start cooking—yes, I have learnt to cook, and rather well too—so I go into the master bedroom and, sitting on the bed in a fluffy bathrobe, open my magazine. I love celebrity magazines. When they are about to come out on their due dates, I literally can't wait. My heart starts beating with anticipation. But recently magazines have ceased to hold their magical allure—a peek into the lives of the rich and famous. I flick through the pages listlessly. I know I am listening out for the sound of the studio door opening. I look at the clock: 5.30.

I get off the bed and go back into the living room. The door to the studio stays firmly shut. I move to the music system and look through his CD selection. I recognize nothing. I whirl around as soon as I hear the sound of the upstairs door open. He stands for a moment at the top looking down on me.

'That was a lovely piece of music. Thank you.'

'You're welcome,' he says, sounding very American. I have come to really like his accent. It is very soft and easy on the ear. He comes down the stairs. 'What are you doing?'

'Trying to find something good to listen to. Haven't you got anything mainstream? Like Justin Timberlake or...?'

I trail away when he winces and looks at me with an expression I cannot quite make out. He comes towards me, rifles through his collection, picks out a CD, puts it into the player, attaches the headphones, and holds the headphones out to me.

'Close your eyes, and listen, really listen.'

'What is it?'

'This is the song I want played at my funeral.'

I become still.

'Go on,' he urges.

I close my eyes and listen. It starts off with a string instrument and then Indian drums followed by English lyrics. Again and again the words, *cannot stay. Despite everything cannot stay.* An Indian voice wailing, but beautifully. *Aaaaaooooooaaaaaa. There's no need to say goodbye. Not even to friends or family. All the memories going round, round.* The voice so full of longing. Again the beautiful wail. *Aaaaaaooooooaaaaaa. The long road. Cannot stay.*

The song is sad on a level that I don't often encounter. I remove the headphones. A conversation starts up in my head. This is too deep. He wants it played at his funeral. Where will I be then? There will be no us then. A strange emotion comes into my body. It affects my entire being.

We look into each other's eyes and something passes between us, like discovering a secret code. Vann inside Julie?   I shrink away from it. Obviously I will be with Jack then. And I feel strong again.   I will not recite the poem to him later.   That would be walking down the wrong path.

I look at him. 'Don't you have Lady Gaga?' I ask.

A veil comes over his face. 'No.'

Twenty-four

Lana is back from her honeymoon. She has invited me to go over to Wardown Towers for tea. The last time I was here was on the eve of Lana's wedding, I had come with Billie and it was already dark, so I had not paid any attention to my surroundings. Now I am sitting in the back of the Bentley alone. I gaze at my surroundings with interest. A guard and gatehouse heralds the start of a long drive that winds through arable fields ringed with wild flower meadows. After about a mile of driving through the estate we passed the long, high brick-walled kitchen garden. Visible in the distance are formal ponds, clipped yew hedges, summerhouses and beds.

At the front door a matronly lady in a gray uniform greets me and takes me through a wing of the house I have not been in before to a greenhouse, the largest I have seen. The roof is V-shaped and it is very old. The floor is made of large stone slabs. Abundant palm trees and the grape vines give the impression of a tropical rainforest. It seems cooler in here. The glass ceiling is lofty. From the open door comes the perfume of honeysuckle.

Lana is wearing an old bottle green sweatshirt and jeans. Her hands are encased in gardening gloves, and she appears to be re-potting a plant. She turns to look at me, and smiles. Even here, standing in an old apron and without a trace of make-up, she looks mind-bogglingly beautiful.

A strange flash of understanding. I like her. I've always liked her.

'What have you been doing to yourself? You look absolutely wonderful,' she says, her voice ringing with sincerity, and coming forward hugs me.

'Hi. You've picked up a tan,' I say shyly, and hug her back.

'I thought we could have tea here since you love flowers so much.' She gestures toward a beautifully laid wrought iron table. Anyway, it's a bit of a mausoleum in there with all the dour paintings and drapes never fully opened in order to protect the artwork.'

'Yeah, I passed a portrait of a stern man with an aristocratic nose and dark, angry eyes. It felt like his eyes were following me around the room.'

'Ah, that must be the founding father of the Barrington dynasty, an astonishingly shrewd and secretive man. Apparently he possessed an unmatched talent for making money. It is said about him that he played with new kings as young misses do with dolls.'

'Oh and what about those two totally eerie stuffed owls?'

Lana's mouth turns downwards. 'Those were pets. They used to belong to some ancestor.'

My eyes grow huge. 'Really? That's what really rich people do. When their pets die they simply stuff them and hang them up as decorations.'

Lana laughs. 'They do have some strange customs. Seems that was where the owls loved to perch when they were alive.'

'I passed a photograph of another of Blake's ancestors in a top hat and tails riding on a giant tortoise.'

'That's the uncle that went mad,' Lana explains. 'He was crazy about animals. He is the one who started the zoo. He once drove to Buckingham Palace in a carriage drawn by zebras.'

'I thought zebras couldn't be tamed.'

'The zebras were led by a horse,' explains Lana.

'I can't believe what we are talking about. Come on, tell me all about your honeymoon. Where did you go? What did you see?'

Lana laughs. 'Blake took me to the desert.'

'That's the great surprise? The desert?'

'Oh, Julie, it was so unbelievably beautiful. We joined an old-fashioned camel train. When it got too hot we traveled in a howdah. It was wonderful. The cameleers were so polite and hospitable. In the day they sing songs; at night they gather around a fire and tell stories.'

She claps her hands together in front of her.

'Blake knew I always wanted to experience rain in the desert, so he had the clouds over us seeded and that night it rained. It was amazing. Truly. We sat at the mouth of our tent and looked at the rain and then we made love in the rain. It was the most sensuous sex I have ever had.'

I look at her and think I must get Vann to have sex with me in the rain.

Something happens outside the greenhouse behind me and Lana is distracted by it. I look over my shoulder and see two peacocks.

'Come on,' she urges. 'It looks like they are about to dance.'

We go outside the glass house and around its side and come upon the peacocks. Lana puts her finger to her lips. We wait a few minutes but she was wrong. Neither spreads its tail. Lana looks at me and shrugs ruefully.

'Oh well,' she says, and we both turn to go back. As we are walking I have an odd sensation. I turn my head and one of the peacocks has opened his glorious tail. I touch Lana's arm. We both turn and catch the rare sight of the spectacular creature dancing for his mate. Strangely my hand is still on Lana's arm. I don't pull it away. When the dance is over Lana turns her bright eyes on me. 'That was spectacular, wasn't it?'

Unable to speak I nod. We have shared something special. I feel connected to her like I have not with any other human being. The piercing jealousy has dissipated.

'Remember that time those boys were chasing me and throwing stones at me?'

Lana looks at me strangely. 'Yes, I do.'

'Why did you come to help me? They could have hurt you.'

'I knew they wouldn't dare. They were afraid of Jack.'

I take my hand away. The old hurt is back. How wonderful for her. To be so cherished and loved and protected by my Jack. 'He looked out for you, didn't he?'

'He was my brother,' she says simply.

He was in love with you, you fool, I want to scream. 'Let's have tea,' I say quietly.

'Yes, let's. You have to try the chef's scones. He makes the most delicious scones I have ever had anywhere.'

We sit at the table and Lana presses a buzzer.

'Does Blake's sister live here alone?'

'Yes, for the moment, but she will be moving in with us when we move into our house next week. She'll only be coming here at the weekends to see her animals.'

'How come there is no information about her on the net?'

Lana lays her hands flat on the table. Her engagement ring glitters. 'Apparently that is what these old families do. They hide the relatives that they are ashamed of or might threaten their social standing.'

'Really?'

'Even the Queen's had two first cousins who were secretly incarcerated in a mental asylum, and Burke's Peerage declared them both long dead, on the misinformation supplied to them by the family. It was only when a journalist discovered in 1986 that one of the women was buried in a grave marked only by a plastic name tag and a serial number and the other is still alive but forgotten that the story came to light.'

The food arrives. Cake stands filled with delicate finger sandwiches, scones, cream cakes and tarts. Lana pours the tea. 'You must try the cucumber sandwiches. Until I came here I had never tasted one. They are exceedingly delicious.'

I take one and bite into it. Lana is right. The cucumber is very finely sliced. It is light and buttery and scrumptious.

'What happened to Victoria?'

Lana's face tightens at the mention of the woman's name. 'She has been locked away in a place where the doors have windows.'

I am shocked. 'Just because she crashed your wedding reception, emptied a glass of wine on your dress and *nearly* slapped you?'

Lana looks directly at me. Her eyes harder than I have ever seen them. 'She had three razor blades taped to her fingers. She didn't want to slap me, Julie. She wanted to shred my face, and disfigure me forever.'

My mouth drops open. 'Oh my God!' The thought of what so nearly happened that day.

'Blake looked like he wanted to kill her that night. I thought he was going to do her harm.'

'It was actually her father's idea. He knew that Blake had become an obsession for her, and if she was not locked away she would do something that would end her in prison. She is being treated with the best that money can buy.'

'Can someone become mad just like that?'

'It seems mental illness runs in her family. Her grandmother suffered a major nervous breakdown and, despite spending many years at a private sanatorium in the care of famous psychiatrists, she never recovered fully. At a grand society dinner party in New York she shocked everyone by eating the roses that were there as table decorations.'

I meet her eyes. 'That makes perfect sense. No wonder she was saying all those crazy things about Blake.'

For the first time since I have known Lana, her eyes become veiled. 'Yes, her breakdown was very unfortunate.'

Twenty-five

As soon as I come into the apartment I know immediately that Vann is not in. The flat seems emptier than normal. I wonder where he is. Perhaps he has popped down to the newsagent. Smith comes towards me and rubs his face against my legs. I pick him up and glance upstairs. Why, the door is slightly ajar. I put Smith back down and go up the stairs.

I even go so far as to touch the doorknob.

So desperately do I want to see the painting he has done of me, but my hand falls away. I can't do that to him. I take a backward step. For the first time in my life I resist my curiosity and refuse to indulge in my propensity to snoop. I run down the stairs and as I get to the bottom stair, Vann opens the front door.

He stops what he is doing and slowly turns his head in my direction. We stare at each other. Not for the first time there is some unspoken message in his eyes. I feel the breath die in my throat. It is as if we are talking but silently. He is telling me something. I am telling him something. I don't trust what I am saying to him. There is something wrong. I drop my eyes. Confused. What the hell just happened? I hear him walk towards me.

'Show me your hands,' he says.

I hold them out to him. 'I didn't look, Bluebeard,' I joke weakly, but my head is still reeling from that silent exchange.

He looks me in the eye. 'I know.'

'How do you know?'

'There are no marks on your hands.'

I laugh. 'Honestly, how do you know I didn't?'

'It's in your eyes.'

I giggle wickedly and start to undo his belt and pants. 'And I...want a thick and tasty treat.'

He likes me to do it on my knees, in front of him. I drop to my knees in obedience and rub his member against my cheek. It feels as warm and polished as a glass sculpture that has been sitting in the morning sun. There are not many things more perfect than this. The moment flips to slow motion and we do it right there on the cool wooden floor with Smith watching from not far away. The movement of his fingers inside me is deft, but raw with sensuality. He stares at me while he fucks me.

'How many licks before I touch your soul?' he whispers.

I am too far gone to reply.

Afterward we both lie on our backs panting, staring at the white ceiling. I turn my face towards him. 'Lana invited us out for dinner.'

'Do you want to go?'

'Why not?'

'OK. Arrange it with her.'

'I have. Wednesday, next.'

'Blake found me an agent. He saw a couple of my canvasses, thought they were good, and has set up a sixteen piece exhibition for me at the Serpentine.'

My eyes light up. 'The Serpentine? Isn't that a really posh place that only showcases the works of the very best artists?'

'Yes, but it's not a reflection of the quality of my work. More a testament to Blake's reach.'

I lie on my stomach and prop myself on my lower arms. 'I hope you're not thinking of refusing. So what if Blake's influence can give you a small leg-up. Everybody needs a break at some time in their lives. If your work is not good enough you'll fail anyway?'

'No, I'm not going to refuse.'

He smiles lazily and I dig my chin into his chest. 'Vann?'

'Mnnnn?'

'Why do you keep your hair long?'

'It's what hair does naturally: it grows. Shouldn't you be asking the other men why they cut theirs instead?'

I pull a face.

He chuckles. 'Hair is not what culture leads us to believe, a cosmetic preference. During the Vietnam War special forces in the war department combed the American Indian Reservations to look for young men with outstanding tracking abilities—experts in stealth and survival.

'But once enlisted an amazing thing happened to these men. The talents and skills they had possessed on the Reservations seemed to mysteriously disappear. Recruit after recruit failed to perform as expected. Extensive interviews and testing proved, beyond a shadow of a doubt, that when the men received their military haircuts, they could no longer 'sense' the enemy or 'read' subtle signs. When the men were allowed to grow their hair back their ability to 'sense' came back. Hair is an extension of the nervous system, a type of antennae.'

'Is that really true?'

He grins. 'Maybe?'

I punch his arm. 'What do you need tracking skills for anyway?'

'To track sulky-mouthed girls with green eyes.'

'My eyes are not green.'

'You keep saying.'

'Vann?'

'Mnnnn...'

'How come Blake's brothers didn't come to the wedding?'

I feel him still beside. Always this reaction when we are discussing Blake or his family.

'I don't know.'

I know instantly that he is lying. 'Do keep in touch with them.'

'A little with Marcus.'

'What's he like then.'

'He changed a lot after his son died.'

There was no mention of that in the websites I had trawled. 'Oh, how old was he when that happened?'

'Eleven months.'

'What happened?'

'Cot death.' He sits up suddenly. I reach out a hand and gently tug him back down. He allows me to pull him back down.

'I'm sorry. It must have been awful.'

'Yes,' he sighs. He turns his face to me.

'Vann?'

'Yes.'

'Do you believe in God?'

'I don't know if I do or not. He gives us so many flaws and then he goes so silent.'

'Do you think Blake believes in God?'

'Why do you ask?' His voice is casual enough, but again his body is suddenly tense.

'Just wondered.'

'Has Lana said something to you?'

'No.'

He props his head on the palms of his hands. 'Have you been snooping again, Julie Sugar?'

I become red-faced. 'I kind of read Lana's notes.' I don't tell him it was her diary.

His face becomes grave. 'Curiosity killed the cat.'

'I'm not a cat. Anyway,' I say, standing up, flinging his clothes on him, and getting into mine, 'I've got to go and practice.'

You see, I am learning pole dancing. Every day I lock the bedroom door and I practice. I am surprisingly good at it since I have been hanging off door ledges doing my Callanetics for years, and I have very strong arms and the suppleness of a gymnast.

Twenty-six

It is a Sunday morning and we have just had breakfast when I turn towards Vann and ask, 'What about BDSM? Are you going to teach me something about that?'

He looks at me over the rim of his glass. 'Why? Are you interested in being a submissive?'

'I don't know. I could be. What is it?'

'It's a game.'

'I like games. Start me off and I'll tell you if I like it.'

He stops smiling, his eyes change, darken. Very deliberately he pushes his glass of orange juice to the middle of the table, reaches for the carton of milk and, holding it right in front of him, slowly tips it sideways until the milk in it pours onto the table. I watch the puddle grow on the table. At some point well before the carton is empty he stops pouring. I lift my eyes from the spill and look at him. His eyes are expressionless, watchful. The silence stretches. I break it. 'Well?'

'Clean it up,' he says.

'What?'

207

'I don't need to repeat myself, do I? It is a punishable offense.'

For a moment I feel confused. Was this the thing that has everybody hot under the collar? Do I want to be his little slave? The answer is obvious and immediate. I don't. Definitely not. But I'll let it play a bit more and see where this game goes. I turn towards the paper towels.

'Not with paper towel.' His voice cracks like a whip.

I turn towards him slowly. Our eyes clash, a look of impatience about his. What does he want me to do? Clean the table with my tongue? The thought is unsexy, off-putting. 'With what, then?'

He leans back and folds his arms across his chest. 'With your sex.'

And suddenly I am wet. The idea is shocking but incredibly, unbelievably erotic. I hook my thumbs into the scrap of white lace around my hips, push it all the way down and step out of it.

'Give them to me.'

I bend down to retrieve them and walk towards him. I look into his eyes as I drop my bunched up knickers into his outstretched hand. He puts them into his trouser pocket.

I hop onto the table with my legs apart so he can see what I am doing, I bend forward and, flattening my thighs, slowly drag my sex across the liquid. Something flashes in his eyes. The milk is cold on my warm skin. When I have swept myself across the spill I stop and look to him.

He nods slowly. 'You,' he says, and there is a touch of admiration in his voice, 'are an excellent pupil. You never do more than what you are instructed to do.'

I say nothing. Just hold myself in that position.

'Now spread your legs,' he orders.

Silently, I open my thighs, sliding them not one by one but at the same time, knees straight and holding them aloft from the table the way a dancer would. My pussy opens out like an oyster, glossy and gooey and unashamedly lewd. Milk drips from the hairs onto the surface of the table.

'Wider.'

I spread out farther. I am so supple I can open wider than most girls. Totally exposed, I wait. The intensity of his gaze makes my flesh tingle. Makes me feel wanton and brings on such an intense craving to be filled and taken urgently that I feel myself creaming right before his eyes, and he hasn't even touched me.

'Spread the labia and show me the pink insides.'

Blood pumps into my clit. I take the plump lips in my fingers and pull them apart, exposing the glistening hole that seems to have a one-track mind. It is desperate to be stretched open, to swallow some rigid meat whole.

He taps his fingers on the table. 'Are you turned on?'

He knows I am, big time. 'Yes.'

'BDSM 101. The game where you are punished for no good reason, and then blissfully rewarded for following instructions and for waiting like a good girl for it. Do you know what your reward is?'

I shake my head.

He sinks two fingers into the soaking folds and, crooking them, begins to stroke that inner nerve that beckons the delicious whole body climax. I throw my head back and moan.

'You like that, pretty puss?'

'Yes, oh God, yes,' I rasp.

He laughs wickedly.

I move my hips so his fingers will enter deeper into my pussy and he suddenly removes his fingers. I open my eyes and look at him. 'Who told you you could move your hips?'

'Sorry.' I have never wanted him more. I look down to his pants. They are bulging with his erection. I know if I touch that rod it will be hot and pulsing. And the tip, my favorite part, that bit that looks like a miniature bum, will be satiny.

'Go and lie face down over the arm of the couch.'

I slide off the table and go drape myself over the armrest. Brazenly I flip my skirt up towards my waist and present myself with my bare ass pushed high up into the air. I try to arrange my legs to be as alluring as possible, think of my bottom as a heart-shaped offering, but it is an odd position—exposed and vulnerable.

Perhaps even a little humiliating. Definitely a ready, begging position.

I am his to ride or do with as he pleases. I feel like a slut, his slut and love the fantasy of it. The loss of control and responsibility for my own body is strangely exhilarating and fantastically exciting. I have the sensation that we are no longer equal, that I have become nothing more than a faceless, anonymous body, an object for his pleasure, to do with as he pleases.

The fantasy of being taken and used selfishly by him makes heat pool between my legs. My own juices are leaking onto my thighs. He doesn't move.

The anticipation is killing me.

Finally, the chair is being pushed back. A delicious shiver. I hear him come and stand over me. For what seems like ages he stands motionless looking down at me. The flat becomes very still. Nothing moves. It is as if time has been suspended. I want to speak, say something, but somehow I know I am not allowed to. I must not move or shift.

'Spread open.'

Two words. Hard like pebbles. I obey instantly. I have to. I have become in the blink of an eye his little sex slave. Now I am splayed open like a starfish with an open pink eye. I feel the air around me move as he bends down and runs his fingers along the wet slit of my pussy and pushes two into the hole. The rush of hot blood into my head is amazing. I feel dizzy as if I am going to climax. My eyes close involuntarily, but he takes his fingers out.

'A Chinese philosopher once said, 'Beat your woman often—you may not know why, but she will.'

While I am trying to get my lust tangled mind around the philosophy of that phrase his palm crashes down hard on my butt. Only when his hand leaves and the cool air touches my skin do I feel the sting and scream. I try to wriggle away. His hands grip my legs hard, not with affection but the way my mother had, once, when I was a child and had unthinkingly tried to run across the road. So hard I cannot move an inch. My cheek is squashed into the cushion.

'A relationship is the opportunity to try out shameful fantasies.' His voice is level, reasonable and so dispassionate that I quit struggling.

He runs his tongue along my spine, kisses my shoulder blade. 'Up to you. Want to see the fantasy through or want to quit now?' His voice is now silky, delicious.

I am aroused, terribly so. At the same time I am not enjoying this new pain aspect that he has introduced, and yet I must see it through for the reward at the end of it.

'See it through.'

'So no more bullshit screaming and pathetic whimpers?'

Gosh, that was a flip. That he can turn his voice so suddenly cold and expressionless. I turn my cheek and look into his face, so close to mine. The eyes are beautiful, unsmiling, unfathomable.

'No,' I say softly.

He moves his face away and I feel his large hands gently stroke the soft burning skin of my butt cheeks. Then it is gone and the next crack on my left buttock is like a jolt of electricity. The air leaves my lungs. I bite the cushion and grunt. Fuck, how can this pain be sexual? My bare flesh is sizzling. I am no longer aroused but more alive than I have ever been. My bum is stinging so much. Tears are flowing from my eyes. Stop, stop, I am dying to cry out, but I don't. It will stop on its own and I will be rewarded.

I begin to count them. Six. The tips of his fingers strike my vagina. I feel an unexpected and powerful spasm go right through me. Seven. I want a repeat of that strike. The urge makes me squirm and rearrange my butt. Eight. But he now confines the spanking to the base of my cheeks. The vibrations drill through into my groin. I am quivering with nerves. My ass is on fire. Concentric circles of pain are radiating out of it. My skin is bathed in perspiration. I'm not going to be able to take much more and yet I am still waiting for another strike from the tips of his fingers. Nine. Maybe he will stop at ten. He must stop at ten. Ten. That's it. Surely that's it. Eleven.

And then he stops. I don't move. I actually feel humiliated. The tears will not stop flowing. But I wanted this. I asked for it, but tears will not stop. I feel used and abused. Feel like a slut or a whore. Even worse, the knowledge that I enjoyed it all—the attention, the pain, the fingers—in a sick, perverted way.

I hear the sound of the foil then his trousers being dropped, and suddenly the tears stop and my pussy opens out like a flower, oil drips from it, and shivers of strange pleasure shoot from my trembling sex. I remain quite still, unconsciously holding my breath as the rounded thickness of his cock forces itself into my dripping cunt.

It is such relief to feel it sinking into me, ending the punishment in the best way imaginable. It is what I have been waiting for. I always knew it would end this way. To be filled like this. I feel complete. I push my pelvis upwards and towards the hot, throbbing cock, ignoring, no, welcoming the pain of brushing my raw tush against his skin.

The ramming my soft center receives that morning.

The friction of my clit rubbing against the sofa mixes with the pain of his flesh striking my sore bottom, and his cock slipping and sliding in the sloppy, creamy excretions makes me ready to burst. Dizzy with erotic pleasure I bite the pillow and sob through the long, rippling climax.

I don't feel him come, I know only my own intense pleasure. My reward. And an amazing reward it is, heightened and illuminated by the raw emotions and beating my little bottom endured that takes me to new textures, heights and depths.

I feel terrified and I feel incomparably and totally alive.

I feel sated and soiled.

Twenty-seven

I take the Tuesday afternoon off and spend the afternoon naked and sprawled on Vann's day bed. As he paints me I watch him. He pouts when he paints. His concentration and dedication to his art is such that I am no longer a person, but an object. But when he finishes, smelling of turpentine and paints, he walks up to me, and with dark, passionate eyes, ravishes me. And each time he has found me ready, a match for his rough needs. I enjoy lying here, my mind drifting, his eyes on me. Being the object of his total attention. My phone rings. Without shifting my body I twist my eyeballs in the direction of the phone.

Lana.

I sit up. Vann frowns.

'I've got to take this.'

'Julie?'

She sounds panicked. 'Yeah...'

'Listen. I don't want you to panic or anything, but Jack has been wounded.'

My bottom drops out of my world. 'What?'

'He's all right. Blake has flown him back home. He's been shot, but he's all right. He will be all right. He's in hospital now. And he's being taken care of by the best doctors. Would you like to see him?'

'Of course.' My voice trembles with emotion. She gives me the address.

I end the call and look at Vann. He is staring at me with a look of almost fear in his eyes. 'What is it?'

'It's Jack. He's been hurt. He's in hospital. I have to go and see him.'

I jump up from the day bed. Vann has my wrist in his hand. 'I'll drive you there.'

I look at him. That sounded fucked up. I experience a pang of guilt. Oh God. I love Jack. What the hell am I doing with this guy? While I have been fucking him and enjoying myself, poor Jack could have died. I step away from him as if he is the Devil himself. I can't help it. 'No, you can't come with me. I couldn't bear it. I feel bad enough as it is.'

He pales. 'You haven't done anything wrong.'

I feel tears start rolling down my face. 'Yes, I have, but that's not important now.' I pick up my robe, shrug into it, and run out of his studio.

The journey to the hospital is one of the worst I have ever had. I should have asked Lana how bad Jack was, where he had been wounded, but I didn't at that moment because I was so shocked, and now I am stuck in the Underground with no reception.

When I get to the hospital, Lana is waiting for me. The sight of her standing there doesn't make me angry; in fact, I feel glad that she is there. I run to her and throw my arms around her. I want to sob, but I can't.

'How bad is he?'

'He was shot in the shoulder, and he lost a lot of blood. He could have died, but he didn't. Blake got him out of there in time.' She shakes her head. 'I didn't know. Blake had a detail on him the whole time.'

My mouth drops open. 'Why?'

'Because he is my best friend.'

I separate from her and sit down on one of the plush chairs. Such a love. Such a love. Even with the addictive foot massages and all the techniques, will Jack ever love me like that? I close my eyes. I feel cold.

'Would you like something to drink?'

I nod. 'Coffee.' I never drink coffee, but I feel like it. I watch Lana walk up to the counter and ask for some coffee. I had thought it would be a vending machine affair, the way it is at the hospitals I go to, but an orderly comes with a trolley, a coffee pot, two proper cups, sugar bowl, milk jug and a plate of biscuits on a tray.

I take the coffee, the cup rattles on the saucer. I take a sip and feel sick. I return the coffee to the tray.

I swallow hard.

'When can we see him?'

'Now. Come.'

She takes off down a corridor and at a door, stops and pushes it open. We go in. The first thing I notice is how pale he is and the second thing I notice is the way his eyes fly to Lana first and then come to rest on me.

'Hi, Julie.'

'Hi, Jack.' I walk up to the bed. 'How are you feeling?'

'I'll live.'

I feel Lana's hand on my arm and I am propelled forward. She pushes me into a chair beside the bed. 'I'll leave you two for a minute. I have to call Blake,' Lana says, and walks to the door. And I experience the strangest sensation. I don't want Lana to leave. I don't want to be left alone with Jack. Probably the guilt. Because of what I have been doing with Vann. All the dirty things I have been doing with Vann. The way I take Vann's cock in my mouth and the pleasure I get from sucking it until he spurts his hot cum in my mouth.

'So what have you been up to?'

Shame flushes my face.

His eyebrows rise. 'So what have you been up to?'

'Nothing. How did it happen?'

He looks away from me towards the window. 'I was careless.' His voice is flat, far away.

'Are you going back?'

'No.'

'Thank God. It's too dangerous out there. You could have died.'

'I could have, but I didn't.'

The way he says it shocks me. Makes me think that he would have preferred to die.

I open my mouth to say something, what, I don't know, and the door opens and his mother walks in. She does not see me; instead she rushes to the bedside with a sob. Jack puts his arm on her hand, and I stand up and walk out. Outside I feel lost. I am not sure which end of the corridor will lead me out of the place. I go down one direction and it leads to a dead end so I turn back. I don't see Lana anywhere so I go into the lift and out of the hospital. Outside the light seems too bright, the noise level too high. I look up and see two very fat pigeons sitting on a roof. I head for the Tube station. I feel shattered. A text message comes through on my mobile phone. Vann. I don't even open it.

When I unlock the door to my room and open it, I am oddly shocked by my own room. How pink and childish it is. It is the room of a five-year-old child. I think of the red satin sheets I have ordered from the Internet. I wanted silk but they were too expensive, so I settled for satin. Vann will wonder what they are about when they arrive at his place. Will he know to put them on his bed or will he leave them unopened?

I look at the wall full of Jack's photos with surprise. He looks more alive in these two-dimensional photos than he did in the hospital. I remember his saying, 'I could have, but I didn't.' What has happened to my Jack? And the despair and grief in his eyes as he turned away from me and stared unseeingly out of the window.

I go and lie on my bed and look at a pink rabbit that I have had for years. What the hell was I thinking of? It is so fucking ugly.

That night there are no stars in the sky. Jack is in London, anyway. I think of Vann in his empty flat. And I feel sad. I won't go back to him again.

I've fucked up. I've fucked up big time.

Twenty-eight

'Ouch!' I cry, and drop the rose stalk. I bring my finger to my mouth and suck it.

'Are you worryin' about your boy in hospital?' calls Ziporrah from the front of the shop.

'He's not in hospital anymore. He insisted on checking himself out,' I mumble automatically, and then I take my finger out of my mouth and look at it. *I was not thinking of Jack.* A drop of blood grows on the surface of my skin. I stare at it without really seeing it.

At that moment I feel as if I had been walking on a road and all of a sudden the road had stopped and I was standing at the lip of an abyss. When I look back the road that seemed so clear minutes ago is dissolving into nothing.

There is no road! There never was a road.

I finish de-thorning the roses, cut the stems diagonally, put them into the metal bucket and store the bucket in a dark corner. Then I clear the tabletop and leave the cool dim back for the sunlit shop. Ziporrah is adding calla lilies into a sophisticated red and dark pink arrangement.

'Zip, do you mind if I leave a little early?'

'How early?'

'Like, now?'

'It's Friday, but we got no deliveries scheduled so I suppose you can.'

'Thanks Zip. I'll make it up next week.'

Ziporrah waves her arms. 'Go, go, go see him.'

I take my mobile out of my apron pocket and dial Jack's number. Jack answers on the first ring. He sounds grumpy.

'Jack, can I come round and see you?'

'I guess so,' he agrees reluctantly.

'Great. See you in twenty minutes.'

Jack's mother opens the door.

'Oh, it's you,' she says. I can't really blame her. I have, over the years, made a pest of myself.

She ushers me into her living room and scuttles back in the direction of the kitchen. Jack is stretched out on his mother's sofa reading a spy thriller. He puts his book down and I find myself a seat opposite him.

'How are you feeling?'

'Bored sick.'

I don't beat about the bush. I don't have time. 'Jack, will you kiss me?'

He shrinks like a touch-me-not. 'Oh, for fuck's sake, Julie, come off it. We've been through this before.'

'It's not what you think.'

'No?'

'No. It's not a sexual thing.'

'Really?'

'Yes, really. Just consider it as an experiment. You can close your eyes.' I pause. 'You can pretend I'm someone else.'

'Why?'

'I just need to know something and I won't know it until I kiss you.'

'OK.'

I grin and stand up. I walk over to the sofa and kneel beside him. He turns his face towards me.

'Ready?'

'Don't talk. Just fucking do it,' he growls.

I lean my palms on either side of him, careful not to touch his body, and gently put my lips on his and close my eyes. His mouth opens and, you know I don't really like cussing, but fuck me, this guy can kiss. His kiss has bells and whistles, and a rounded tongue that expertly snakes around mine, hooks then pulls it into his mouth, and gently sucks it. I feel myself getting lost in the sheer beauty of his kiss. It is romantic and sexy, the way I always think kissing a film star might feel, but raw sexual heat—nada, neinte, zilch, rien. Nothing, nothing, nothing. I move my head away.

He is looking at me expectantly. 'Well?' Nothing for him and nothing for me.

'Thanks, Jack. You've been a great help.' I grab his cheeks between my palms and smack my lips loudly on his forehead. 'Got to go. Get well soon,' I say and I run out of the door.

Outside I am so exhilarated I want to jump up and scream. How could I even have thought that what I had with Vann could be replicated with anyone else? Only now I realize how special is the chemistry I share with him.

I rush home, call a greeting out to my mum and run up the stairs. I close the door, look at the wall of Jacks and laugh. What a total fool I have been. I've been so focused on being in love with Jack that I did not even realize that I've fallen in love with Vann. I change into my red dress, the one Vann loves, apply a layer of red lipstick and I run out of my home.

At the Tube station I cannot help smiling to myself. At my stupidity. At my happiness. I imagine what Vann will do. I know he likes me. I know he likes me a lot. I smile foolishly. An elderly woman meets my eyes and lets hers slide away quickly.

'It's OK, I'm not mad. I just found out I'm in love,' I tell her.

She smiles. It is not a London fuck off and leave me the fuck alone smile. It is from the heart.

I open the door of the building Vann lives in and run to the lift. At the lift my bag catches on the stair banister. My bag falls, opens, things spill out. I crouch down to pick them up.

Fate is a strange thing.

Whether you turn right or left when you walk out of your front door can change your life forever. I don't know how the future might have played out if my bag had not caught and the contents spilled out. But those few seconds meant I look up and see Lana coming through the doors.

She appears distracted. She sees me and comes up to me.

'Hi, Julie. Are you coming or going?'

What, I wonder, would have happened if I had said coming? Instead I say, 'Going.'

She looks relieved. 'Shall we do lunch sometime next week?'

I feel anger in the pit of my stomach. What the hell are you doing here? Is the billionaire not enough for you? This is my man.

'Yes, let's.' I press the lift button. The doors open immediately.

She steps in. The cheek of the woman. She smiles at me. I smile back automatically, but fucking hell is she having an affair with my man? The doors close on her and as if I have winged ankles I race up five flights of stairs. I stand at the fire door, breathing hard.

When I get my breath back, which occurs surprisingly fast, I march down the corridor. I take my shoes off and turning my key, quietly slip into Vann's apartment. I tiptoe to a little alcove that leads into the living room, and crouching behind a cupboard watch them. What I hear is nothing like what I had expected!

'I love him so much. I just want to help, but he won't tell me anything,' Lana is saying. Her voice sounds distraught and desperate.

'It is not because he does not want to tell you. Nothing that happens in the circle can be told outside it.'

She paces agitatedly, coming in and out of my line of vision. 'Can he step out of the circle?'

'There is no escape. The circle has no end. Besides, he would not want to. Coming out would put you and Sorab in grave danger. He makes his sacrifice gladly.'

'Can I enter the circle?' Her voice is a whisper, full of terror. It makes my hair stand on end.

Vann's reply is instantaneous. 'Never.'

What the hell are they talking about? Suddenly, I remember the crazy notes I saw about the brotherhood of El. And the unbelievable things that Victoria had screamed about.

'What must I do then?' Lana asks desperately.

'The fight between good and evil is as old as time. It will never be won by either side. Involving yourself will bring great personal loss to you.'

'Should I do nothing, then?'

'No matter what you do, the brotherhood will carry on holding their great balls for El. You will not be invited. Neither will I. Blake will always be invited as an honored guest, but he won't go... Because of you. Because of your love for him from outside the circle.'

'Loving him from outside the circle doesn't stop the nightmares.'

'Nightmares?'

'Every once in a while when he has had a particularly stressful day he has a nightmare. Then he screams out in the voice of child. He told me that the memory is blur and dream-like, but when he was a small boy he took part in a ritual and killed another child.'

'The first rule of control is to hijack history.'

'What do you mean?'

'Blake didn't kill anyone. The child that is being programmed usually never does. It just wakes up alone from a drugged state with a bloodied knife and a dead child. And then it screams and whimpers for its mother for hours.'

'How do you know this?'

'Because when I was seven years old I stumbled upon the ritual. I accidentally got locked in the same room where the ceremony was being performed. I saw what they did. I saw his little body stiffen up when he was being stabbed. I felt dirty for not looking away. When they left it I sat frozen for hours. When the other boy awakened and began to scream I wanted to come out and comfort him, but even then I knew that if I showed myself I was dead, and the instinct for self-preservation is strong even in a child. But the shock was incredible. It changed me. The world became a frightening place. There was no one I could trust after that. I always knew they did that to both Marcus and Blake.'

'They never did it to you?'

'No. I was never the right material. They choose their victims very carefully.'

'How do they choose them?'

'That knowledge will not serve you.'

'Is there anything else you can tell me?'

'The rest cannot be told. Only remember that they want you to believe he is like them, but he is not. He never has been and he never will be.'

'I've been doing some research on them, and—'

'Don't.'

'Don't what?'

'Stay away from them. They have existed from time immemorial. They will be here when you and I are gone. You cannot defeat them. When you gaze at something long enough you become it. Even what you fight, you become. Keep away from it. Stay pure. What they hate more than anything else is a pure heart. When you are pure they cannot touch you. And the longer that Blake gazes at you, the purer he, too, will become. You are not here to take them on. You are here to protect your son and every child that your charity can reach. Go and tell Blake he did nothing wrong.'

'I will.' Lana walks up to him and, standing on tiptoes, kisses him on his cheek. 'Thank you, Vann.'

He says nothing, simply looks at her kindly.

She goes to leave and then turns back towards him. 'Have you told Julie who you are?'

'No.'

'She may seem like an air-head sometimes, but you can trust her. I would.'

She walks to the door. When the door clicks shut I come out of my hiding place and stand in the entrance of the room.

'Who are you?' I ask, but I already know. Of course, I know. It should have been obvious to anyone with eyes. I should have known from the first day.

Invictus

And yet the menace of the years
Finds, and shall find me, unafraid.
                    —William Ernest Henley

Twenty-nine

I, Quinn Adam Barrington

'You're Blake's brother, aren't you?' she accuses, her voice, a shocked whisper.

She is wearing scarlet. I love her in scarlet. I can hardly remember her from the days she used to dress in shades of pink. She has changed so much. Her hair is loose and she is wearing red lipstick. In the glow of the light from the lampshade her creamy skin glows with the luminescence of the polished ivory sword handle that had hung in my father's study.

She is my beautiful love. My heart feels heavy. Why didn't I tell her myself? Something has always held me back. I know why. I know exactly why.

I incline my head. 'At your service.'

'Why didn't you tell me?'

I shrug. To tell her would be to leave me defenseless.

She smiles suddenly, brightly, and advances into the room. 'It doesn't matter, I realized today that I love you,' she says excitedly.

I freeze. I actually freeze. Now I know why I never told her. But I thaw surprisingly fast. There is no pain. Maybe later. Definitely later, I will think of those words and how much I wanted them to be true. Now I am like the man whose shoulder is inside the lion's jaws. The pain is so great that shock cracks a whip, and a weird flat state of being takes over; it is notable only for its total absence of pain. I always knew she was shallow, but this shallow? Not even I could have expected that.

'Why? Because I am not from a family of servants you have suddenly decided that you love me.' My voice is bitter. I have never heard it so. So much about me she has brought forth.

She frowns then turns white. 'You heard us.'

'Yeah. I came to say goodbye, but after hearing how scornfully you dismissed me just because you thought I was the son of a servant, I walked away.'

She licks her lips. Her eyes turn desperate. I look at them emotionlessly, curiously. How far will she go?

'It's not what you think,' she pleads. 'I knew I loved you before I figured out that you are Blake's brother.'

I raise a disbelieving eyebrow.

'I came here to tell you.' Her voice is rising, desperate.

I say nothing. I wanted her to love me for myself. Not for my family name. But I have been living in a fool's paradise for the last few weeks. I so much wanted to believe that she is more, that she could be more. But what I feared most has happened.

'You have to believe me.'

'And what about Jack?'

'I realized that I didn't love him this afternoon and that is why I came here.'

'What an amazing coincidence.'

'I'm telling the truth, Vann... I mean...Quinn.'

Wow, she is a really good actress. 'Don't call me that.'

'Why don't you want to be known as a Barrington?'

'I wanted to be recognized as an artist, purely for my talent, not because of my surname and heritage.' I'll never tell her the real reason why I don't want to be associated with the name.

'I love you.'

I laugh. 'Well, I don't. We had a good time and now it is over. I'm leaving at the end of the week.'

She takes a step back as if I have slapped her. Her eyes become huge. She is right though, they are not green. Flecks of gold and brown in them. They are only green when passion comes into her body.

'You're leaving?' she gasps. Her mouth remains open. This is not acting. This she did not expect.

'Yup. I'm done here.'

For a few more seconds she simply stares at me. I long to cross the space and hold her, but I don't. I stare at her, my beautiful Sugar. Then she turns around and runs from me. She doesn't slam the door, but closes it quietly with a click.

I close my eyes and take a deep breath. I stand there, my thoughts a mess. Some part of me tells me to go after her. Let things carry on as before. But another part of me knows that it can never be like it was before, and whatever we have will be a pale imitation of what I really want. It is for the best. I don't want her to pretend to love me. I need to be free of the long shadow cast by Jack. A song is playing in my head. Mama, take this badge off me. I can't use it anymore. I feel like I'm knocking on heaven's door. Knock, knockin…

The phone rings.

I answer it and listen as Blake explains that he has ordered Croix, my dealer, to put a minimum price on the paintings: £150,000 on the smaller ones, £250,000 on the two larger pieces. These giddy prices… The arrogance is breathtaking.

Abyssus abssum invocat: one hell summons another.

Here it goes again—the meme that money is absolutely everything. I am reminded of Munch's *Scream*. His terrible visions, profound insight and his shudder of despair at the human condition reduced to a price tag: 120 million dollars. The hollowness had chilled me then. And it chills me now.

In ordinary circumstances I would have gone mad, told my brother to fuck off, stay out of my business. But today it doesn't matter. I don't actually care one way or another.

'Nobody will buy them at those prices,' I say quietly.

'I am the back-up buyer at those prices.'

There is a brief pause when we are both silent.

'You are the artist. I am the businessman. Leave me to decide what the market can afford. The perception of value is everything. If a Barrington wants to acquire the entire collection...'

'You haven't seen it yet.'

'Is it any good?'

'The best thing I have done in my life.' I slept with my muse, you see.

'That's good enough for me.'

'See you tomorrow at seven thirty?'

'See you then.'

'Oh, do you need us to pick Julie up?'

And suddenly the pain hits. Right in the solar plexus. Oh fuck. Later has come.

'Yeah.'

'Right. I'll get Lana to arrange it with her. See you then.'

The phone hits the wall so hard it smashes into pieces. I stand with my back to the glass wall and look around me. Here, I have been truly happy. I go to the kitchen and open the fridge. That habit of hers, leaving a half-drunk glass of orange juice in the fridge. I take it, find the imprint of her mouth and drink a mouthful of juice. The juice is cold and for some reason tasteless. I leave it on the counter. I need a real drink. I reach for the bottle of beer and stop. I don't want beer. I'd like to get smashed on a whole bottle of cognac, the kind my granddad used to drink. I close the fridge and I go up to my studio.

At the threshold I stand and look at the empty place. By now, all the paintings are probably being unpacked and the perfect wall to hang them on being decided upon. I go towards my easel, my paints and my brushes. They have comforted me in other times of pain. But not pain like this. I walk to the unfinished canvas on the easel and look at it. There she is smiling mysteriously at me. I put my palm on her mouth and drag it down the canvas. The wet paint smears downwards. I take a rag and wipe my hand and walk to the tap. I watch the water running and realize that the large ceramic sink is totally out of place in this state-of-the-art apartment. It occurs to me that Blake had it installed.

He wanted it to be like my studio in Paris. He went to a lot of trouble, quietly. But I have never appreciated him. I wash my hands and go downstairs, cross the silent, empty space and enter the bedroom. The bed is unmade. I go to Julie's side and smell the pillow. There's her scent. Is it mango or coconut shampoo that she uses? I lay my head on the pillow.

My eyes fall on the lap dancer's pole. As if the scales have fallen off my eyes, I understand now that the previous tenant didn't decide to leave, he was told to leave, or rather given an inducement to leave. In his hurry to accept, he left the pole behind.

She was practicing her dance for me. I will never see it now. I stand and, like a man in a daze, go to it. At the level of her crotch I sniff it, but it smells of metal and lemon polish. I let myself lie on the floor and stare at the ceiling. For a while there is the sensation that I am the last man on earth.

That I am totally alone.

Thirty

Julie Sugar

I walk to the Tube station numb with shock. It had all gone so disastrously wrong. In the train I stand with all the other passengers. A man in a pin-striped suit stands up to offer his seat to a pregnant lady. I watch the exchange blankly. She sits and meets my eyes. Smiles. I smile back automatically. At my stop I scramble off. I stand on the platform for a moment before heading towards the exit. I put my ticket through the barrier gates and come out into the silver light of the evening. There is dog poo in my path and I manage not to step into it. I open my door and my mother calls out, 'Is that you, Julie?'

'Yeah, it's me,' I reply and I am surprised by how normal my voice sounds. I go up the stairs and enter my room. I sit on my bed and look at the wall of photos. I see Jack smiling up at me, squinting, looking moodily, laughing, expressionless, a cigarette dangling from his lips, sitting in front of a beer, and the photo I never liked, but kept anyway—a girl on his lap and two kissing him on either cheek.

Strange.

How very strange.

Is it possible that even this morning I had kissed Jack's photo and been convinced that I was in love? I had built a fairy tale in my mind and I was so strong-minded that I refused to give it up, no matter what. Now I know I must have been mad to think that I was in love with Jack. What a fool I've been? I feel the bitterness of my own stupidity. I sit with my hand pressed to my midriff. Could I trust what I feel now? And yet the feeling is worlds apart.

I loved Jack in my head, I loved him because he had the blue eyes, because he was so handsome and so dead cool and because all the girls were crazy about him, and what a trophy it would have been to have him, love him, because he was a doctor and in the end he was an imaginary figment of my imagination.

I love Vann with my entire body and my heart. I love talking to him, I love being in his presence, I love kissing him and being kissed by him, I love making love to him, I love the way he makes me wet simply by looking at me, I love eating with him, I love listening to music with him, I love having a laugh with him, I love that he doesn't give a shit about money and celebrities.

I love that he doesn't strive for what all of us spend day and night trying to acquire—oodles of money. He simply walked away from it all without a backward glance. What most human beings would sell their souls for. What I felt for Jack is a tiny thing compared to what I feel for Vann. My entire body feels it. I realize, too, the feelings I had nurtured for Jack were all wrapped up in jealousy about Lana and wanting everything she had. I feel light-headed and suddenly cold. It is like being in a dream. I thought it was passion and lust but it is love. Things that shouldn't make sense do.

I'm in love with him.

I am head over heels in love with him.

How long have I been in love with him? I cannot say. It does not matter anymore. Only that I love him. The depth of this new yearning is so intense, the ache so great that the girlhood crush that I nurtured and stubbornly kept alive for years has paled into nothing. He is the first person to make me 'feel'. He makes me feel replenished. My fears have flown. I no longer need to gorge simply to hang my head down the toilet. I took him for granted. Never appreciated the splendor of the man.

Surely he must have felt something for me too. I think of him, winking at me, building me up in that dim drawing room, accepting me into his flat that first night even though he had heard me refer to him so scathingly as a servant, asking me to pretend he was Jack, crouching beside me on the toilet floor and wiping my damp face as I stank of vomit, offering to take me to the hospital to see Jack. Why, no man would do that if he did not love a woman to distraction!   I've hurt him terribly.

How crazy life is. There I was thinking he is ashamed he is poor and it turns out he is ashamed that he is immeasurably rich.

I walk over to the wall and begin to take down the photos. One by one, the memories of where I had acquired them, when I put them up. God! How very silly I have been. I stand on a chair and pull down the highest one. I pick them up and put them on a pile on the bed. The wall is stained with Blu-Tack marks. I want to tear all the photographs into tiny little pieces and forget I was ever so mad and foolish, but I cant. I've had them for so long they are a part of me. They tell their own story. The story of how I allowed a crush to become an obsession.

I sit on my bed and realize that I must tell Vann everything. Everything. I can win him back. I won't give up. I will go with him to Paris or Provence or wherever the light is best. He will paint and I will go to the open-air market for vegetables and fish and meat. We will have a wooden table where I will prepare everything. The windows will not be slash. They will open out; perhaps they will have shutters. I will cook and we will eat together and make love, and we will be happy. In winter we will light a big fire and watch the snow falling, making everything vanish in white.

My phone rings. It is Lana.

'Hi.'

'Yeah.'

'What's the matter, Jules?'

'Nothing.'

'You sound a bit down.'

A sob rises in my throat. I swallow it down. It remains a lump in my throat. 'I'm all right, really.' My voice sounds funny.

'Look, Blake won't be back for another two hours. Why don't you come over? Do you want me to send Tom or would you rather take a taxi, my shout if you do?'

Now the tears are running down my face. 'I'll take a taxi, but you don't have to pay for it,' I blubber.

'Oh, Julie. Would you rather I came to you?'

'No,' I sniff. 'I'll come over.'

I go to the mirror and watch myself cry. I am one ugly fucker when I cry. The phone rings again and Lana says, 'Don't take a cab. Tom's very close to Kilburn and he is already on his way to you. He'll call you as soon as he gets to your block and you can go down to him, OK?' Her voice is very kind and it makes me want to bawl.

'All right,' I sniff.

I don't cry in the car. I simply sit staring out of the window. How strange that the one friend I seem to have in the world is the person I thought I hated. I arrive at the wide, tree-lined street, manned on either end by armed diplomatic Protection Group officers. Set back on the eastern side is Kensington Palace. Here, too, is where the

Russian Embassy is located and where the steel magnate, Laxhmi Mittal, lives. This is London's billionaire's row, Lana's new residence. Each mansion is white stone and surrounded by spacious gardens, but I don't see anything. Tom drives us into the gated magnificent mansion that is Lana's new home.

I get out of the car and Lana herself opens the tall front door. She comes down the steps and taking me by the hand leads me into the house. I look around me, dazed. It is as beautiful as a palace. Even in the daytime a massive chandelier, hanging from the lofty ceiling, is blazing with light, and the floor is gleaming like a mirror. She takes me into a sumptuous sitting room full of all the usual trappings of wealth, but I am too upset to pay any attention to them. Sorab's toys and a coloring book are on the floor. As if he had been there moments ago.

'Come sit down,' she says.

'Where's Sorab?'

'Gerry's taken him outside for a bit. Thought you might like some privacy.'

I nod. A woman in a black and white uniform comes in. She smiles and nods in a friendly fashion.

'Do you want anything to drink or eat?' Lana asks me.

I shake my head mutely. Any food would make me hurl.

The woman nods silently and leaves. Lana guides me to a deep sofa and sits beside me. 'What's the matter, Julie?'

I look into her beautiful face, take a deep breath and say, 'I've hated you for years.'

She moves back as if struck, her hands falling away from mine with shock.

I plough on. 'And I've been envious of you for even longer. You see, I fancied I was in love with Jack but he only wanted you, so I was jealous, rabidly so. I think I also became a bit obsessed with you. When I was younger I even sometimes prayed that you would drop dead.'

'Oh.'

'And that's not all. When I came to your apartment the last time, I looked at the notes beside your laptop, and on your wedding day I went into your room and read your diary. And I'm really, really sorry because I realize that you've never been anything but good to me and I've been such a selfish, shallow bitch.'

She clasps her hands in her lap and for a moment says nothing, and then she looks up at me, her eyes are twinkling. 'Did you read anything interesting in my diary?'

I smile tremulously. 'I didn't get a chance to read too much. You came back into the room.'

'And you hid in the cupboard.'

I gasp. 'You knew?'

'A wisp of your dress was trapped at the bottom of the cupboard door. It could only have been you or Billie. I kinda figured it was you. Billie would have chosen to dive under the bed.'

I laugh then. Not a happy laugh, but a relieved laugh. I should have done this years ago. Unburdened myself. It feels so damn good. I finally feel clean.

'Now tell me what is wrong?'

'Just now, when you went to see Vann, I was not going, but coming. I sneaked in after you and listened to your conversation.'

'Why?'

'I don't know. It was crazy but I thought you were having an affair with Vann.'

Lana stares at me speechlessly.

'I'm sorry. I don't know what came over me. I know you love Blake to bits. Anyway, I confessed to Vann that I am in love with him, but he refused to believe me. He thought I was saying it because I had just found out he was a Barrington. He'd come upon us talking at your wedding reception, and heard me refer to him as a Barrington family servant so he refused to believe I could be in love with him if he wasn't rich. But I swear it on my life, Lana, I don't care whether he is a billionaire or hasn't got a pot to piss in. I truly love him.'

'When did you find out you loved him?'

'I knew I was in love with him when I went to Jack's mum's house this afternoon and asked him to kiss me as an experiment... And felt absolutely nothing. What will I do, Lana? He says he's going back to Paris.'

'Don't give up Julie. I know he cares.'

The words 'Don't give up' resonate. A memory resurfaces. The only thing that had never fit was the fatherless thing, but if Vann is Blake's brother then he *is* fatherless. 'Oh my God, the fortune-teller was right.'

'What fortune-teller?'

'The one at your wedding.'

Lana laughs. 'That was just for fun. I didn't think she was particularly good.'

'What did she tell you?'

Lana makes a face like, How obvious? 'She told me I'd found my soul-mate and I'd have three kids, two boys and a girl. And she told me not to go swimming on my own after the age of thirty-five. Otherwise, she saw bright and happy life ahead. What did she tell you?'

'She told me not to give up on a strong, tall, fatherless man. She also told me evil was trying to touch me and I must not let it. She didn't elaborate and even more intriguingly she made me give her a coin so I wouldn't owe anything. As if she was afraid me owing her would somehow taint her.'

Lana's face changes. The secrets come back into her pale face. Now I am dealing with the woman who wrote the diary.

'What do you think she meant?'

'I don't know, Julie. If you heard my conversation with Vann, then you will know I know hardly more than you.' Lana takes my hands in hers. 'But Vann is right, there are many things hidden that are best left hidden.'

'Lana, why were you always so nice to me when we were kids?'

She shrugs. 'Don't know. For some weird reason I always wanted to as a sister.'

'Really?'

She nods. 'Are you still coming tomorrow for the art exhibition?'

'I don't know if he will want me there.'

'He does. Blake offered to arrange your transport and he agreed.'

'Really? He does?' My heart feels like it would burst.

'Yes, really. Have you got something to wear?'

'Most of my clothes are a bit tight now. I'll go shopping tomorrow.'

'Shall I arrange for some cocktail dresses to be sent over here and you can come around and pick what you like?'

I stare at her in disbelief. Would I like to? 'Hell, yeah!'

She smiles. 'Got any color preferences?'

'Yeah, red.'

Thirty-one

Do you know the only thing that gives me pleasure?
It's to see my dividends coming in.

—John D. Rockefeller

Darkness has not yet fallen when Tom comes to pick me up. Billie is already in the car. She smiles at me.

'You look amazing,' she says.

She says it like she means it, and I blush with pleasure and wonder what it must be like to be kissed by a woman. All soft lips and silky skin. 'Thank you, Billie. As it happens, I don't think I have ever seen you so beautiful.'

And it is true. She is dressed in a mini silver dress that is covered in tassels. Every time she moves all the tassels agitate, shimmer briefly and settle down. She looks almost molten.

'It's a present from Lana.'

I nod. Of course it is. For the first time in my life I feel nothing but warm love for Lana. I am not in competition with her. She has Blake and I don't have Vann, but maybe I will. Maybe the gypsy knew something I don't. I won't give up hope.

Tom drops us off at the Serpentine gallery. I feel incredibly nervous. The sky is shimmering with myriad colors. As I step out a woman comes up to the car.

'Miss Sugar?'

'Yes.' She is wearing perfume strong enough to cut through steel. Once I doused myself in that way too. Once, when I was a different person.

'Come this way. You are the guest of honor.'

Billie winks at me. 'Go on,' she says. Once I would have gone. Skipped away and left Billie to her own devices, but I am different now.

I hold my hand out to her. 'Where I go, you go.'

Billie grins. We walk together through the entrance. There are so many people, and they are all so finely dressed.

'You're cutting off my circulation,' Billie whispers in my ear.

I relax my fingers. 'Sorry.'

'No problem.' She smiles. 'It's just that I kinda like having fingers.'

That makes me smile.

Vann is coming towards us.

Billie gently unknits her fingers. 'You'll find me at the bar. I'll be drinking up the place.'

I can't even turn my head to look at her or make any kind of answer. Oh my! How gorgeous can a man look? I have never seen Vann in a tux before, and he is simply magnificent. Without doing anything he dominates the room, simply with his presence alone. I watch him walk towards me, his gait unhurried, deliberate, confident. A lion roaming the savannah. And yet, when he stands before me, he appears ill at ease, his eyes without laughter or life.

'You look very handsome,' I say softly.

'Thank you. You look exactly how I imagined you would in an evening dress.'

He doesn't elaborate further, but I blush like a schoolgirl.

A waitress appears with a mirrored tray bearing a selection of canapés. She waves her free hand towards them and tries to tempt us with creamed, piped anchovies, lobster mousse, or even blue cheese with poached pears.

Even the thought of food makes me feel ill. Both Vann and I politely decline. A waiter comes by with flutes of champagne and both Vann and I reach for them immediately.

Vann looks at me. 'You are the star. Don't get drunk.'

My head rears back. 'I'm the star?'

'Yeah. I want you to see the collection before it opens to the public. Come,' he says, and, laying his hand on the small of my back, guides me towards an area sectioned off with red ropes. With an untouched drink in my hand I follow him into the viewing area.

And blink.

That's fucking me! On that canvas. And... I am beautiful beyond anything I have seen in the mirror. Not beautiful as a human being is, but as an image can be. And... I am much, much larger than I really am. And yet I am luxuriously, gloriously beautiful. I remember his words. *You will be desired, cherished and possessed for the very things you are ashamed of.*

How can I describe Vann's art to you? Only to say it is what all great art should be—beyond words. Indescribable.

I stand there shocked.

There is only one word for my state of being. Overcome. As I move from canvas to canvas, Vann my silent shadow, I don't gasp or exclaim or utter a word. You see, I couldn't make a single sound. Until the day I die I will be glad I never made a sound. A sound would have broken the magic language of his art. For Vann has woven a vivid story that speaks to my soul.

Amongst the dabs and strokes of color, I see Blake, I see Smith, I see flowers, I see skulls, I see robed Chinese horsemen, and snakes and cranes. I see Yehonala, and I see *me*. I see me everywhere. In every painting: there I am, eyes glazed with passion, or dreamy, or angry, or hard, or sly. Standing by the window, the sunlight streaming in, throwing the colors and patterns of a large, open, semi- transparent fan onto my breasts.

And I see Vann.

In each wild, joyful splash of color I see his dreams, his desire for freedom. It is everything that matters to him, everything worth giving up what he once called 'the unyears' for. I feel proud of him.

Skulls, snakes, evil-looking flowers, but all have been transformed into objects of terrible beauty.

In one painting a baby, its eyes open, is in a jar. Fragmented pain vibrates across the canvas as if the painting itself is crying. You can't just hang *that* on a wall and not look at it. It screams at you to look at it, experience it—it's terrible beauty. It is like the lure of Medusa.

As I pass through I notice that all his paintings have a lyrical longing that is fraught with something darker. Sometimes it comes in the way of horns where none should be. Sometimes in the form of sharp cornered black cubes or the single eye, suspended and watching. I remember—the symbol for the brutal God El.

Finally, we come to the last piece, the pièce de résistance.

I can't take my eyes off it.

And you must bear with me now because I *have* to describe it to you. It is unbearably erotic and sublimely beautiful in execution, but there is something else. A something that almost feels as if the painting is alive and it is gently purring at you. The undercurrent of mystery and emotion that powers out of it is like a palpable energy. It makes my stomach clench. It reminds me of the feeling I had when I was reading Lana's notes. The uneasy sensation that hidden away from my view, in the dark there are things that I know nothing of.

In the painting I am sitting in a garden, and the garden is so lush and so dreamy that the viewer will convince himself that it must be Paradise. I am nude, sitting with my legs wide open, head tilted slightly, mouth parted, and eyes mysteriously hooded and inviting: it is a brazen invitation to whoever is watching to enter me. But they won't dare. A very large cobra is coiled around my body and my legs. Its hood is extended and its mouth aggressively open. It is a fierce guard. For my sex.

I remember his words, 'Beauty is dangerous. It has the ability to tantalize and crush. Even strange beauty.'

The painting is titled *Adam & Eve*. It would seem that I am Eve and the cobra is Adam, but— here's the occult gem: Vann's real name is Quinn Adam Barrington. At the bottom there is a little card: Not For Sale.

I don't turn to him and say the work is beautiful, because that would cheapen it, judge it, classify it. Let it be left that his art left me speechless.

'My art didn't come out of a vacuum. It came in a flash... After you. Thank you.'

I turn to look at him. He looks unbearably sad. I want to put my arms around him, but I know it will be the wrong thing now. Later. I have plans for this man. I don't know what is in my eyes, but he takes a step back from me.

'Let's go back out. I'll introduce you to everyone.'

I nod, and we leave that area and go back out amongst the glittering people. Lana comes to me. She is wearing a jaw-droppingly large, pink diamond teardrop pendant necklace. After she gets pulled away I smile and nod, and smile and nod, but I am not the same person who came in to see the exhibition. All I can think of is that last painting of Adam and Eve. The expression on my face, the exaggerated plumpness of my mouth, the ferocity of the Adam between my legs. Vann tries to keep me with him, but I can see that all these people want to talk to him, have a piece of him. Some of the women even give me dirty looks. They want the newborn star, and they think I am monopolizing him. After a while, the dirty looks become tiresome and I allow myself to be separated from Vann. My feet take me back towards the paintings.

His paintings make me remember what I thought I had forgotten from my school days. A snatch of Oscar Wilde. *To reveal the art and conceal the artist is art's aim.*

I start again at the beginning, but now, with the other people shuffling about me and their quiet murmurs dotting the air, the effect of his paintings are thankfully less intense. My senses are not as overwhelmed as before, and I can assimilate more. I hear snatches of their conversations.

'The colors remind of Ed Baynard's *Flowers That Talk* range, but the background is almost Murakami.' A woman declares that they are 'scary but compelling the same way a road accident is. Horrible but it makes you look.' A man with a pompous voice makes me stop and listen. 'It's good, but there is too much slavish attention to beauty.'

He is exactly the kind of intellectual snob who would declare a tin of excrement as an innovative piece of great art. Vann has done what he set out to do—beauty is no longer a frivolous thing, a pretty postcard or a chocolate tin Monet painting. Beauty, he is saying, can be compelling the way horror is. You don't want to look at a skull of an evil-looking, flesh-eating flower, but you have to because it is so beautiful. He has become the master of beauty, strange beauty.

A man comes to stand beside me. 'So, you're the muse.'

I look at him. He is in his thirties and brilliantly successful in some capacity that would make him useless on a desert island. But here, he is a prince holding two glasses of champagne. He is the kind of guy that would install a lap dancer's pole in his bedroom.

'Sam Shepherd,' he introduces. 'What will they say? Not a toilet bowl in sight.'

I smile despite myself. How Vann would laugh. I will tell him later about this remark.

'The last painting is...interesting, isn't it? Do you think it has some hidden meaning? A social commentary on our dissolute life? Or...' His eyes suddenly change. They start to undress me. I am frozen by the violence in his eyes. Nobody has ever looked at me like that. 'Would you like to have your purse full of money and supper with me in Paris?'

Suddenly Vann is at my side. I exhale the breath that I was holding in a rush. Sam smiles at Vann.

'I was just asking Miss...' He turns to me briefly. 'Sorry I didn't quite catch your name, what the meaning of this painting was.'

Vann's jaw is set in a hard line. He doesn't smile and he looks angry. I realize that I have never seen him anything but indulgent or passionate. This new Vann is perplexing. Messes with my head and yet I kind of like that he has this side to him. This hard, don't mess with me persona.

'It is exactly what you think it is.'

'I'd like to buy it.'

'It's not for sale.'

'I am prepared to pay more, far more than the price the others would stop at.'

'It's not for sale,' Vann repeats tightly and curling his fingers around my upper arm starts to turn away.

'Three hundred thousand.' His voice is loud. I realize for the first time that he is drunk.

Vann is already walking away with me in tow when another voice, a thin, reedy one, farther away, says, 'One point five million.'

There is a gasp.

Vann stops and turns around to look at the owner of the voice. Everyone else does the same. A small, slim man. From head to toe he is dressed entirely in black. His face is thin, pointy and deathly pale, and his eyes are deeply sunken and glitter like dark gems. He is tiny and insignificant, but I am suddenly frightened of him. I cannot explain the immediate and instinctive fear. I feel Vann stiffen beside me. For a long, tense minute there is pure silence. That old cliché, you could have heard a pin drop, became true.

Then the air around me moves and Blake is standing next to me. From him come waves of antagonism for the newcomer and a rock-like, unshakable support for Vann. I feel Vann relax and some of my fear sloughs off like old skin. It is the most amazing feeling, having someone like Blake in your corner. You know that, no matter what happens, he is going to come out the victor.

'Monfort,' Blake says coldly.

Monfort acknowledges the greeting with a slight, silent bow of his head. His mouth curls at the end. And there is something evil about that grotesque curl. I shiver.

'Congratulations. It is a fine painting Mr...Wolfe. It does us proud.' The hesitation is deliberate. He knows. He knows that Vann is a Barrington.

'Thank you.'

'You have my offer if you do decide to sell.'

Vann nods.

He turns his attention to Blake. 'Your father would have been pleased with you. Come and see me in the cigar room.'

'If time permits.'

At that moment I know it is absolutely true what Vann told Lana: *The brotherhood will carry on holding their great balls for El. You will not be invited. Neither will I, but Blake will always be invited as an honored guest.*

The man called Monfort moves the tip of his mouth into a cruel curl. His dark eyes settle on me. 'I bid you goodnight, Miss Sugar.' Then he turns and slips away, a silent, black shadow.

'Well done, Vann.' A look passes through them and Blake smiles at his younger brother. There is so much in that smile. Vann visibly relaxes and around us the crowd starts whispering and moving and everything becomes normal again. Lana pushes through the crowd. Her brow is creased with worry and fear.

'Is everything all right?'

Blake catches her by the waist and playfully growls, 'Of course. Except for the fact that you are not by my side. Where have you been?'

'I got waylaid by this woman who wanted to talk about CHILD.'

'The penalty of success is to be bored by the people who used to snub you,' he replies with a low laugh.

For a moment Lana looks from Blake to Vann to me, and back to Blake. Vann shrugs, I shake my head, and Blake grins innocently.

'Fine,' Lana says with a laugh. 'Don't tell me, then.'

Thirty-two

'Are you cold?'

I shake my head. I am burning up.

He releases my hand. 'Let me call you a cab.'

'Take me home with you.'

'It's over, Julie.' His voice is flat, final. He never calls me Julie. I am Sugar to him. But you know me. I don't give up easy. No one can accuse me of not trying.

'Can we have sex one last time?'

He starts to shake his head.

'Then why did you do what you did in there?'

'Because he would have destroyed you.'

'What makes you think he wanted me? I am white trash from the council estate.'

'Snoop Dogg is not black. He's Snoop Dogg. You are not Julie from the sticks but Eve from the painting.'

It gets suddenly colder. A cold that eats into bone. I hug myself. The sickness of my need for him grows, like moss on my skin. 'Do we always remain who we are, no matter how much we try to be someone else?'

He looks at me sadly. The realization is swift. He has already walked away from me. But I won't give up. The gypsy woman said not to. 'Why is *Adam & Eve* not for sale?'

'Because it's yours,' he says simply.

'Don't you want it?'

'No. I want no memories of you. You can sell it. Buy a little flat like Billie's.'

I just about stop myself from wailing. But I don't want a little flat like Billie's. I want to live with you in a garret in Paris or wherever. Is this how it ends? The thought is impossible to comprehend. The pain spreads from my chest outwards.

'You're leaving. What harm can it do for us to spend one last night together? I came to your exhibition. Don't you want to see my dance? I practiced hard.'

He says nothing.

I wrestle with the entirely futile desire to reach a hand back into the past and change it. If only I had not been so obstinate. So hateful. 'Please.'

'If you keep the story going long enough, it will always end badly for all the characters,' he says.

I know I am begging, but I don't care. I touch his arm. 'It will be my goodbye dance. You can't deny me that...'

He takes his jacket off and drapes it over my shoulders. 'All right.' The jacket is full of the delicious warmth of his body and I snuggle into it. It is another expensive gift from Blake. We don't speak at all during the walk to the car, in the car and on the way to the front door. He puts the car keys on the table. Smith comes to greet Vann. His fur sticks on the black material of his trouser legs. He bends and rubs his head affectionately. I walk on ahead, take his jacket off and carefully drape it over the back of a dining chair. The flat smells of flowers. There are baskets of flowers everywhere, the congratulatory envelopes still unopened.

'Want a drink?'

'No.'

'I have green chartreuse.'

My eyes open wide. What? When did he buy that? It can only be a good sign. I let my lips stretch in a smile. I'm in love with a handsome devil. 'In that case, I'll have a glass.'

I go and sit on the sofa and watch him pour the drink out for me. His shoulders are tense. Hardly meeting my eyes, he approaches with a glass of something amber and my drink.

'What are you drinking?' I have never known him to drink anything but beer.

'Brandy.'

He sits on the same sofa, but there is at least a foot between us. One lousy foot. I can scale that. I bring the drink to my lips, aware that he is now watching me, and take a small sip. Shit. It tastes like cough medicine. I cradle the glass in the palm of my hand.

'Why did you buy it?'

'I don't know. I saw it on the shelf of a shop and I just had to.'

'Just had to?'

He sighs. 'Just had to. Do you like it?'

I wrinkle my nose. 'No.'

He laughs softly. Not the beautiful, irresistible rumble that comes from his abdomen, but I rejoice anyway—it's the first since I confronted him. 'It's OK. You have to be ninety to enjoy it.'

The moment of lightness passes very quickly.

'Finish your brandy. I want to have a quick shower and change into something more appropriate,' I say, standing up.

He simply looks up at me with darkened eyes. For a moment I stand looking down on him. Someone once said, love is like wearing shoes that fit perfectly. He fitted. Perfectly. From the first moment I tried him on. But by mistake I took him off and someone has accidentally put him back into the shop window and now I'm terrified someone else might come along and take him.

I reach down and touch his lower lip. He belongs to me. Mine and only mine. Another day he might have sucked my finger. This night he does nothing, simply stares at me. I feel my loss. A sense of vertigo. I straighten. I'm not beat. I haven't even started yet. *He will forgive me.* I will dance and crawl for him. Tonight I will be Yehonala.

My legs begin moving. The click of my heels is loud in the silence of us. I feel his unreadable eyes on my back until I am swallowed by the angle of the wall. I will use tonight the way it is meant to be used.

I take off the sexy little strappy dress that Lana and I chose together and hang it behind the door. Then I shower and dry my body so briskly it glows. I look at myself briefly in the mirror. My tummy is still toned and flat, but now there are curves, lush curves. I shimmy my shoulders and my breasts dance prettily. I turn and look at my rounded bottom. It's become a handful. I remember that day he kissed it and declared it sinfully sexy.

'It makes my cock throb like mad,' he said. The memory is clear. But to be honest, I am not obsessed by what I look like anymore. I had nothing in those days. So I obsessed about my looks and Jack. Tonight I only care that Vann will like what he sees. Tonight I am a vase. To be filled and used.

I brush my hair and leave the glossy curls carelessly tumbling down my back. *Tonight will see me painting my body...for you.* First, I adorn my mouth with scarlet, bracelet my body in a red bikini, and then I tie a red velvet ribbon around my neck, tight enough so it constricts my throat slightly. With a brush and black eyeliner I draw a mole to bewitch just above my top lip.

But when I look at myself in the mirror, I see nothing but the too tight ribbon, a strangely erotic gash of red. It tells its own story: the tale of a selfish, shallow girl who became a woman at the hands of a selfless man—a man who put her pleasure before his own.

I pull on the new thigh-length black boots that I picked up from Camden Town and tie the black ribbons that hold them in place.

Now we will see if what he has taught me is enough to seduce the man I want.

I slip on a toweling robe and cross the silent flat.

Thirty-three

Neither do people light a lamp and put it under a bowl. Instead they put it on its stand, and it gives light to everyone in the house.

—Matthew, 3:19

I stand in front of the door of the master bedroom, left slightly ajar. Take a deep breath and push it open. The lights are dimmed. He has taken off his bow tie, opened some buttons, and is lying in bed waiting for me. He turns his face to watch me. For a moment I am floored. He has made the bed with the red satin sheets that I ordered.

I close the door and flick on the fourth switch from the left. A spotlight illuminates the pole. His eyes swing to the pole then back to me as I walk to the stereo system. My CD is still there, on top, untouched. I slip it in and walk towards the bed. His gaze is locked on me. I was sleeping before he came. I am awake now. Unsmiling, I let my robe slip from me and fall around my boots.

There: there: that leap of desire. He wants me. That is what I needed to see. That live ember in the dying ashes.

The music comes on. *El tango de Roxanne.*

First the piano then the dramatic wails of the violin. A loud clap. More melodious violins. Then the voice, more raspy than sandpaper snarls: *The man who falls in love with her. First there is desire. Then. Suspicion. Then. Anger. Betrayal. Jealousy, yes, jealousy will drive you, will drive you, will drive you MAD!* I begin to walk towards the pole, my stride as strong and sleek as a Spanish dancer. A temptress.

I reach the pole and, as the throaty rasp roars *Rooxannnnne* I execute a perfect cartwheel and grasping the pole hard, throw myself into such an energetic low spin that it makes my hair fly into my face. I land on my legs open wide, almost in a crawl and facing the pole. Flipping backwards, the palms of my hands flat on the floor, I use my legs shaped into a V to hook and pull myself back onto the pole. With both hands I begin to climb it.

You don't have to put on that red light.

Every time my hands move up to grasp the pole and pull myself upwards, my head and neck dip downwards like a ripened stalk of wheat in the wind. The movement, I know, I have seen, is elegant and full of beauty. It is like ballroom dancing—all the grace comes from the dips the dancer makes before he takes his next step.

You don't have to wear that dress tonight.

I get to the top as the singer's scratchy howl fills the air...*Roxannne.* I squeeze the steel between my thighs, the cold metal pushed into my pussy, and high in the air above him, I fling my hands out and let my body fall backwards into the air, my spine straight, my head upside down, my hair a waterfall of curls.

You don't have to sell your body to the night.

For the first time since I began on the pole our eyes meet, lock. It is dark where he is, but what I see makes the breath leave my chest. There is a look in the rebellious Barrington's eyes that is starving hungry, but something else too. Something dark and raw. An intense desire blazes forth that cannot be resisted and refuses all attempts to rein it. Any effort to do so will bring insanity.

His eyes tell me I am a goddess. That he had not expected such intensity, such strength or such skill. His eyes move away from mine, boldly roam my body. Slowly, deliberately I pull my body upwards and I stop thinking about him. I concentrate only on the music while I make love to the pole.

His eyes upon your face.

I twine myself around the pole and, with the same sinuous movements a snake makes, slip and slide down the pole until I sink to my knees with the pole against my back.

His lips caress your skin.

I stand and, holding onto the pole seductively, with pointed toe, high step around it. Just when he thinks I am going to push my ass up into the air and sway seductively, I flip my body over and touch the floor before grasping the metal tightly with both hands and lifting my legs clean off the ground. My body is now in a spread-eagled position perpendicular to the pole. Held purely by the strength of my hands I start spinning slowly around the pole, my legs held as far apart as the hands.

It's more than I can stand.

As the music builds and picks up speed I increase my speed, the air rushing into my face, my legs scissoring the air, the knees bending, the legs moving upwards, all the while spinning faster and faster and suddenly I am upside down and still spinning like a top.

Why does my heart cry?

A whole orchestra of violins and cellos goes crazy in the most dramatic and sweeping ballad of the entire piece. I execute a turn with a bent knee and maneuvering myself upright on the pole begin the journey up the pole, the same deliberate dip and rise.

Just don't deceive me.

At the top I prepare for the finale. I split my legs wide. Hold that spread position, with only the tiny strip of wet red net fabric to cover my opening, and wait for the perfect movement. When it comes I loosen my grip and begin my free fall head first. It is like the death drop. Even over the music I hear him gasp.

And please believe me when I say I love.

Two feet from the floor I squeeze my thighs on the pole and halt my drop. I am face down and perpendicular to the floor, held by my strong thigh muscles and the strength of one hand, the other outstretched over my head. At the sudden clash of cymbals I release my hold on the pole and fall flat on my face to the ground. Silence. Then. Guitar. Violin.

Slowly, I begin to roll towards him, pausing every time I am on my side. Like Cleopatra rolling out of a carpet towards Mark Anthony. The music grows and grows. Every movement I make is deliberately submissive, designed to captivate, like the animal that offers its throat to its mate. I reach the foot of the bed.

The timing is perfect. Many voices mingle to form the crescendo.

Roxannnne, Roxaannnne...

I am panting. Not just with exertion, but with need and desire. He appears at the edge of the bed and wrapping his large artist's hands around my ribcage pulls me up, very much as one would do a mermaid from the ocean, onto the bed.

'I need to get my mouth on that wet, unbelievably delicious pussy of yours.'

'How do you know I'm wet?' I pant, on my back.

'Because, my little puss in boots,' he says very softly, sliding my knickers down my legs and dangling the little red thing, 'I saw this...' And clearly I see the wet patch in the gusset. A small shiver goes through me. 'And became very hungry for pussy butter.' He goes to put his mouth between my thighs, but I palm his throat, as he had done to me on our first night.

'No, this one's on me,' I say, and lifting myself up change positions. I straddle him; sit on his chest, on his good shirt. *It is not sex, it is attention, it is flattery—that is what no living man can get enough of.*

I shift down and unbutton his trousers. He is wearing white briefs.

'White underpants? You know I can't resist you in white underpants,' I breathe.

A lone pulse beats in his temple. God, how could I have been so stupid? All the while my real feelings for him were staring at me. All the while I was falling deeper and deeper and my own stubborn stupidity kept me focused on Jack.

I bend forward and take him into the hot wet cave of my mouth, and suck the shaft in so deep there is nowhere else for him to go. What could he do but buckle and explode deep in my throat? Slowly I begin to unbutton his shirt. Expose the warm skin.

'You blew my mind...' he says, and expertly unclasps my bra. Sweat has glued it to my skin. He peels it off and my breasts pop out. He rolls the nipples between his fingers. 'But I still need to get my mouth on those voluptuous pussy lips.'

I rise to my knees, straddle his chest, and push my crotch towards him. My pussy is so tantalizingly close to his chin he can surely smell my arousal. I look down at him. 'What? These old, swollen things?'

He eyes my crotch greedily. Inside my boots, my toes curl with anticipation.

'They do look a little...erm...used.'

'Used and bitten and ravished. Three times a week.'

'Come and sit on my face.'

I walk on my knees up to his mouth and suspend my sex over his mouth, the inner folds exposed, throbbing, and silently screaming for release. I am buzzing inside. Secretions of lust leak from me as if I am a faulty tap.

'Don't be gentle with her,' I command.

He flicks his tongue out and I raise my hips out of reach. He grabs my hips and pulls me down onto his mouth.

'Ohhh...' My head falls back. The silky warmth of that dexterous mouth. The suction. The suction. It is killing me. I begin to sizzle inside. My fingers grip the headboard as if my life depends on it.

'Oh God. Oh Vann...' And I can no longer hold on. I grind into his teeth as the orgasm overwhelms me, my skin tingling, my mind a white flare.

'Too soon,' he growls and tumbles me over. He sits up. 'Onto all fours.' I right myself and obey instantly, my inner slut mewling. I hear the sound of the foil.

'Don't.'

He pauses.

'I'm on the pill.'

For a second I feel his naked head against my soaked opening and moan and then my cunt becomes a sheath for his cock, as he grabs my hips with both hands and ruts and rides us both home.

Fucked, my cunt in a spasm, I fall forward and hear his ragged breath as he falls on top of me. Our bodies are slippery. I grip my muscles hard to keep his seed inside me but it trickles out helplessly.

'God you're beautiful.'

'I don't need to be wooed.' My voice is hoarse, a stranger's, my breathing viciously quick. 'I need to be taken. Again and again.'

And that is what he does. Again and again. Until the night sky becomes pale and we are both so exhausted we curl up against each other and sleep.

Thirty-four

First gather your facts, then distort them at your leisure.

—Mark Twain

I watch him sleeping.

The lines that held his face so tightly last night are all relaxed. He looks so beautiful I want to weep. He opens his eyes. They are soft and slumberous and not yet attuned to the world. He whispers my name.

'Julie.'

A smile ghosts my lips.

For an instant there is silent communication between us. An odd moment that we are both caught in it... A string of connection—like the first time our eyes met. When I was a bridesmaid and he the best man and he winked at me across a crowded church. Then he deliberately breaks the moment and, turning away, sits up. He pushes his hair away from his forehead. I squeeze my eyes shut. I won't give up. I open my eyes and, reaching out a hand, touch his back. He stiffens.

'Julie...' he starts to say.

I sit up, the sheet falling away from my body, and clamp my hand across his mouth. His eyes travel down to my bare breasts. 'Before you say anything else I want to show you something.'

He blinks and nods.

'Thank you.'

We get dressed, get into his car and drive to Kilburn. I ask him to stop outside my house. We go up the stairs and down the corridor without exchanging a single word. My stomach is in knots. I am so nervous I feel like throwing up. In front of my door I stop and put my key into it. As soon as I open the door the stale smell rushes out, engulfing us. I look up at Vann. His face tells me everything I need to know. Shock. Disgust.

'This is my house.'

He swallows. I take him to the living room. My mother is too shocked to stand or speak.

'Vann, this is my mother. Mum, meet Vann.'

Vann moves forwards and takes her soft swollen hand in his.

'Come,' I say to Vann and take him upstairs to my room. I unlock the door. 'This is my room.'

He follows me into my scrupulously clean bedroom. I turn around and watch him close the door, lean with his back to it, and look around him. His face is carefully blank.

I point towards the wall with the bits of Blue tack still sticking on it. 'That wall there used to be full of photos of Jack, some even blown up to poster size, but I took them all down the day before yesterday. I wanted to tear them all into tiny pieces, throw them away and pretend I had never been so stupid, but when it came to it I didn't have the heart. It would have meant that I wasted so many years of my life. They're in that drawer.'

I point to the lowest drawer of my dresser. His eyes follow my finger. He seems bemused.

Here goes. Total honestly.

'I kissed Jack on Friday.'

That makes his eyes jump back to me. The cobra rears its head fiercely.

'I called him up, went to his house and asked him to kiss me. And he's a good kisser, I'll give him that, but you know what? I felt nothing. Absolutely nothing.' I look pleadingly into his eyes. 'Vann, you're the one I think of all day, you're the one I respond to even when I don't want to. You're the one I love. That crush I had on Jack was based on hot air. It was just a fantasy created by a lonely, terribly, terribly unhappy girl.'

He opens his mouth to say something, but I hold my hand up.

'There are other things you don't know about me. I'm not a good friend to Lana. When you met me I was jealous of her and I hated her, or at least I thought I did, but the real truth is I hated myself. I hated everything about me.

275

'Remember you once asked me about my dad and I didn't want to talk about him? Well, my dad was a drunk. "You are nothing but an animal," my mother would sneer as he walked through the door, and it would all kick off. He would hit my mother and my brother, but never me. He loved me. Sometimes when he was very drunk he would fall on the couch and lift one arm so I could climb in and the arm would come back down. It was warm and nice in there.

'But one day after a particularly furious bust-up my mother packed a suitcase and we left home while he was still asleep. They temporarily housed us in a bed and breakfast on Cromwell Street. It's gone now. They pulled it down and built something else, but then it was full of other broken people like us; prostitutes, asylum seekers, single mothers and their children.

'We were having breakfast when my father walked through the door. He was swaying. His eyes were large, glassy and haunted, a drunk's eyes. "I've come for Julie," he said. My mother did a strange thing. She looked at me with cold, strange eyes and tight lips.

"Let her choose. Do you want to stay with me or go with your father?" I looked at her. At how cold her eyes were and I said, "Stay with mummy." My father turned around, stumbled and walked away. I think I regretted my decision before he was out of the door, but I didn't do anything about it. I never saw him again, until I was fifteen and we heard he died in a ditch. I've never forgiven myself for that decision. I should have gone with him. He needed me. She didn't. She had my brother. She would have gone on just fine without me.'

'It's not your fault, Sugar. He was a grown man.'

'And one more thing. Don't think you'll have changed my life by giving me that painting or that you can wash your hands of me that easily, because I'll never sell that painting. It will be with me till the day I die. If you really want to change my life I suggest you take me with you wherever you go.'

'Will you come with me to Paris?'

I am so shocked my mouth falls open. 'Say that again,' I whisper.

'Come with me to Paris.'

'Really?'

He smiles.

'So you *do* care for me.'

He puts out a hand, pulls me towards his hard body, and starts kissing my neck. 'Care?' he murmurs. 'How blind can you be? I'm crazy about you, Sugar. I have been since that first night. It was a knife in my heart to know that all the time you were with me you wished you were with him.'

'My poor darling. I'm sorry I was so cruel. Sometimes I would feel it, those invisible strings pulling me towards you, but I was so insanely obstinate, I'd break them by mentioning Jack. The truth is I was only reminding myself because I had forgotten him.'

'I even started to hate the guy.'

'Will you ever forgive me?'

'There is nothing to forgive. I love you.'

It feels as if my heart is going to burst out of my chest. His lips trail delicious kisses along my neck. 'I can be a bit slow on the uptake. So,' I pull my neck away from him and look into his eyes. 'I want to know everything. Tell me what you felt from the first moment we met.'

'When I saw you for the first time in the church, I could hardly believe my eyes. I had spent years travelling the world looking for something that would fire my blood and bring my canvas to life, and there you were totally unaware of your beauty. I had already decided to ask you to dance when I got an even better opportunity thrown in my path.

'It was like fate saying, 'here have this.' But when I came to find you to say goodbye, I heard you refer to me as the son of a servant, and I thought, maybe I had been wrong. I certainly never expected you to turn up, so when I heard your voice on my intercom it shocked me. I thought to myself, play this cool Vann. And I did until I gave you a forkful of my mash and saw the way you ate it, I knew then you were starving, for food, for attention, for love. From that moment on there was no more resisting you. That night I was not teaching you how to be Yehonala. I was Yehonala and you were the Emperor. I had one night with which to impress and captivate you.'

'You sure did that. I was astonished. The things you made me feel. You made sex beautiful.'

He chuckles. 'The beautiful way you owned that pole last night?'

I am suddenly shy. 'That was a bit brazen, wasn't it?'

'Totally.' He grins. 'I'll be wanting a repeat performance tonight, by the way.'

'You have to deserve it,' I say with mock severity.

'Let me see. How about my agent told me last night that I've got a Getty Center commission for a series of paintings in the same vein?'

'Oh! Wow! I'm so proud of you.'

'I couldn't have done it without you, Sugar.'

'Vann?'

'Mnnnnn.'

'Who is Monfort?'

He sighs heavily.

'You are afraid of him, aren't you?'

'Yes.'

'Why?'

'Only a fool with nothing to lose would not fear them. They know no boundaries.'

'Why is Blake not scared of him then?'

'Because Blake *is* one of them. In the strict hierarchy of the brotherhood Blake is far more powerful than Monfort, but because Blake is moving away from the agenda he is open to challenges. His love for Lana also means that he has become vulnerable. It is how they get everybody—find a weak spot, exploit it. But Blake walked away the winner last night.'

'But you told Lana, it is her love for him that is saving him.'

'With or without Blake the agenda will be implemented, but because of Lana and his love for her, he has discovered the humanity that he lost to the brotherhood.'

'What is the agenda?'

'Why do you want to know?'

'It has to do with the deliberate poisoning of the earth and the extinction of mankind, hasn't it?'

For an instant he looks surprised. 'Lana's diary?' he hazards.

I nod. 'Why? Don't they, their children and their grandchildren have to live on this earth too?'

'The answer is staring you in the face. They always hide everything in plain sight. Think. What is the one movement that is more inexorable and unstoppable than anything else? It pervades the entertainment industry, politics, military 'breakthroughs' and scientific circles. No matter who you are or where you are you will be exposed to it. You see it in commercials, music videos, movies, and hear about it being discussed at the highest levels.'

I frown. 'I don't know.'

'You watch music videos all the time, don't you?'

'Yeah.'

'Lady Gaga, Will I Am, Jay-Z, Beyonce, Rihanna... What do all their slick videos have in common? What do they glamorize?'

In my old life I would have said, awesome designer clothes, catchy tunes, fantastic dance moves, and brilliant choreography. The new Sugar knows: it is not those things.

I shake my head.

'Don't give up so easily, Sugar. This is a little test to see how successful the controllers have been.'

The clue must lie in the names he has given me. I try to think with the destruction of the planet in mind. Lady Gaga coming out of an egg, Beyonce wearing riot police gear, Will I Am with his robot themed videos and Rhianna flashing the one eye symbol—come to think of it all of them flash that.

'The coming police state and robots?'

'Bravo to the brotherhood.' There is no joy in his face. 'The coming superhuman is disguised as a courageous and exciting project, but its true implications are vast and horrifying. Just like splitting the atom can go both ways. There is no desire or quest to 'evolve' all humankind. If there was then the one percent of the population wouldn't own more than half of the world's wealth.

'The true aim is to alter the human genome to survive under a toxic sky, as two species; the new homo-superiors, in reality, the homo-predators and what is left of a successful depopulation strategy—the genetically engineered and chipped slaves. The agenda in a nutshell is the quest for godhood, to live for hundreds of years and rule with unchallenged domination.'

'Do we do nothing at all about it, then?'

'What do you want to do, Sugar? Tell everyone? They would only brand you a fruitcake or a conspiracy nut. It is as I told Lana: what you fight you become. Are the Inquisitors better than the witches they burnt? The real battle is inside you. If every single person on earth refused to lift a gun, propel a drone, hurt another human being in the name of democracy, or 'freedom', or whatever shit they call their murderous ways, this world would be a paradise.'

Finally, I understand the confusion and vulnerability Lana had shown in her notes. *I am afraid. Hold me*, I want to say, but I don't because I don't want to taint my happiness. No, no, I won't react now. I will think of it all tomorrow. I can unravel it then. Tomorrow is another day. Now I will just love this man with all my heart.

Still, I must have looked mournful for he caresses my cheek, and says, 'The only thing we can really do is live our life to its fullest. We may be among the last of the humans to live and die on this world.'

I smile softly up at him, relieved that he is not Blake. He doesn't have to constantly watch his back. Lana is braver than I. I don't know if I have the strength to risk my man to machinations of sinister men like Monfort.

In the car I call Lana. She sounds sleepy. 'Don't go swimming alone after you turn thirty,' I tell her.

For a moment there is silence. Then she gets it and there is bubble of laughter. 'Oh! wonderful. I'm *so* pleased. Is he with you now?'

'Yup.'

'OK, tell me everything later, but we go out to dinner next week.'

'That will be brilliant.'

'Speak to you soon, babe.'

'Lana?'

'Yeah.'

'I love you, you know.'

'We were always meant to be sisters.'

Lana Barrington

Invictus
(Unconquerable)
It matters not how strait the gate,
How charged with punishments the scroll,
I am the master of my fate:
I am the captain of my soul.

I end the call and smile. Stretching deeply I roll over and bury my face in Blake's pillow. Ah! The smell of my darling's head. It's Sunday. The chef has his day off and Blake makes breakfast, I cook lunch, and we order in, or go out for dinner. Early Sunday morning is Blake's time with Sorab. I lift my head and hit the button for Kitchen on the baby monitor. Blake's voice is tinny on the monitor. He has no idea that I often lie in bed listening to his monologs. Crazy guy, he is talking to his fifteen-month-old son about his business deals.

I look at the time. It is still too early to call Billie.

I am dying to hear what happened between her and Jaron Rose. He surprised me. Billie had described a man she found in a club where everyone was off their cakes on drugs, and given me to believe that he was a rough and ready lad, who had taken her to an unremarkable, badly furnished flat, but the Jaron Rose who came to the exhibition was dressed in expensive clothes, hand-made shoes and spoke in a posh voice. And when he spoke to me he had come across as highly educated and suave. In fact, he was so sophisticated, charming and mysterious, he reminded me of James Bond. As if he might have been a debonair spy or something.

'So what do you do, Mr. Rose?'

'Please, you must call me Jaron.'

'Jaron.'

'Property,' he said with a knowing smile. 'I buy and sell property.'

'Is the market good at the moment?'

'Dazzling.'

He was so smooth and debonair that for the life of me I could not imagine a man such as him going to a club like Fridge and picking up girls with spider tattoos running up their necks. He was also with someone, a woman who draped herself possessively around his broad chest and looked daggers at Billie when she was introduced, but I saw him before Billie did, and the look in his face. He looked, as Billie would describe it, as if someone had pushed a cattle prod up his ass. And what of that fire of wild joy that briefly lit his eyes.

He took Billie's hand and held it for seconds longer than polite society required. Enough to pass on its own message.

'It's been a long time.'

'Has it?' Billie replied coolly.

'Sometimes you win the lottery and lose the ticket.'

'Faint heart never won fuck all,' Billie retorted sweetly.

'Introduce me, darling,' the woman with him urged. Her voice was honeyed but there was a warning there, a deadly one. I am absolutely certain it said, 'Behave.'

A shadow passed over his eyes. For a second he looked like a damned soul. 'Of course, darling. This is the inimitable Billie. Billie, meet my fiancée, Ebony.'

'Charmed, I'm sure,' Ebony said sweetly, but her eyes clearly said, this is my turf. Go away. Get your own.

I get out of bed, brush my teeth quickly and go down the stairs. Every time I come down these fantastically grand stairs I almost cannot believe that I live here. That this is my house. That it is actually in my name. I cross the marble floor and make for the kitchen.

Sorab is sitting in his high chair and watching his father with big eyes. Blake is beating eggs. They both turn to look at me at the same time and my heart swells with pride. My beautiful boys.

First I kiss my son. 'Good morning, darling,' I say, then I go up to Blake and kiss him. 'I love you so much.'

'Show me how much?'

'I'm not dislocating my arms this early in the morning.'

He laughs.

'Lana.'

We both turn towards Sorab and then look at each other with astonished faces.

'Did he just say "Lana"?' Blake asks.

I laugh excitedly. 'I can't believe it. Other children start with babbling and my son calls me by my name.'

I go to Sorab and put my face level with his. 'Mummy,' I say.

'Lana,' he repeats loudly.

'Stubborn little thing, aren't you?' I pick him up, all warm and sweet-smelling and nuzzle him. He smells of milk. One day this smell will be gone. I dread that day. 'Julie called. Good news. Vann and she seem to have ironed out their differences.'

Blake cuts a bit of butter and puts it into the pan on the stove. 'You think it's a good match, don't you?'

'Made in heaven. What are we doing today?'

'Feel like doing a bit of sunbathing?'

I put Sorab back into his high chair. 'What?'

'We are going to the Île de Groix for the weekend.'

'Since when? I'm not prepared.'

'All you need is a bikini and some toiletries. Gerry will meet us in the plane in two hours. Tom will be here in an hour.'

'Are you serious?'

'I never kid about important things.'

I shake my head in wonder.

'Come on. It'll be fun.'

'Do you ever wonder what life would have been like for you if Rupert had not taken me to that restaurant that night?'

He shudders. 'Don't even go there.'

I walk up to him and push my body up against his. His reaction is instant.

'You're hard!'

'And you're wet!'

'What're you going to do about it, then?'

'You'll see, after I've charmed you with langoustines and champagne and when you're on your back on the sand, the sun beating down on your naked body, and the waves lapping against your legs.'

'Mnnnn... I can smell the butter starting to burn.'

He doesn't move away, simply grins and snatches the pan away from the fire ring.

I stand on my tiptoes and kiss the tip of his nose. 'Why don't you go out into the garden with Sorab and I'll make breakfast?'

He strokes my throat, his eyes passionate and fierce. 'Until I met you I never knew anybody who was...pure. You will never understand what would have happened to me, what I would have become

if we had not met that night, because you are too good...too pure to understand. And even if I try to tell you, you will not believe me.'

'But we did meet,' I tell him with a smile.

Outside the sun is shining brightly.

"Within thirty years, we will have the technological means to create superhuman intelligence. Shortly after, the human era will be ended."

Vernor Vinge, Technological Singularity.

Maintain humanity under 500,000,000 in perpetual balance with nature

—Georgia Guidestones,
http://en.wikipedia.org/wiki/Georgia_Guidestones

Bonus Material

POV

Blake Law Barrington

I knew something was wrong. I knew the way you know someone behind you is staring at you. A prickling. I began to sprint towards the marquee, faster and faster. Even before I got to the entrance I heard Victoria's voice: she was screaming hysterically. Some slow moving part of my brain—but she's not invited. Through the crowd, I saw Lana, standing with her hands held loosely by the sides of her ruined dress. And her face... Oh God, her face: white, slack about the mouth, beaten.

Utterly devastated.

I felt like a man who was coming out of a thirty-year coma. Disassociated from my frozen body, but aware of the crash of my heart, the roar of my blood in my ears, and the demon sucking at my belly.

I had only been gone for a few minutes. It was breathtaking how effectively and easily all my

careful planning had been laid to waste. Lana's disgrace could not have been more complete. How happy she had been only a few minutes ago.

My immediate and instinctive reaction was to run to her and spirit her away from the mess that was our wedding, away from the eyes of all those mean-eyed, cut-glass accented parasites gathered around her, all whom I know were secretly happy to see her humiliated.

I hated them ferociously, then.

But the cold part of me, the one my father had ruthlessly nurtured, told me that that was not the Barrington way. Here, in the scene after the bullet had struck, and the deer had sprinted its last stumbling yard and collapsed with the final hush of all things, I had to put my hand into the hat, and pull out, not the crows that took flight at the sound of the gunshot, but the deer before it jumped, froze with terror, and ran, while mortally wounded. I had to restore my love to her earlier brilliance.

I took a deep breath and walked into the situation. I willed my legs not to, but they quickened anyway. I couldn't stop them striding to get to her faster. I saw Quinn put a protective arm around her shoulder. She did not respond to his touch.

She was looking with wide, unseeing eyes into the crowd. She was looking for me! Tears came into my eyes. Because of me she has been hurt her again. My head felt like it was underwater, but I was breathing fire. I bit down on my guilt.

I'll make it right again, I promised.

Finally, I stood before her.

Quinn took his hand away, and the gawking horde of self-satisfied simpers dissolved into inconsequential shadows. She raised her shocked gaze up to me. We locked eyes. She was mortally wounded, but still breathing—still breathing. I saw clearly her shame, her desire to slink away and hide. She was begging me to hurry her away from her disgrace. But there would be no running and no hiding for us. My wife would stand taller than them.

'She'll never stop, will she?' she gasped. Her eyes were huge, like those of a child who's been slapped when it has done no wrong—wounded, confused and frightened by the world around it.

'No harm can befall a single hair on your head while I am alive.' My voice did not come out choked with the anger and horror I felt. It was a show of power and impregnability. That encouraged me. I took her hands in mine and metaphysically let the strength inside me flow into her.

Tears filled her eyes and shimmered precariously at the rims. 'My dress—' she whispered hoarsely.

'Can be recreated to the last stitch. Remember...' I reminded tenderly. Then I simply gazed deeply into her eyes with all the love I felt for her. You're my heart, my life and my whole world, my eyes said. Can't you see that all of this is nothing? None of it matters. There is only you and me and our love. I'm besotted with you. All these people could disappear tomorrow and we would still be happy. Who cares what they think?

She stared at me. Did the layers of impressions press through? Maybe. The color was coming back to her face. She blinked, and the tears that were brimming in her eyes, spilled over. With one finger I gently wiped first one cheek and then the other.

'Thank God for waterproof mascara,' I said.

She sniffed and offered up a ghost of a smile.

'That's my baby,' I said, and raised my hand. It was the cue the organizers understood. Instantly, all the lights cut out except for the twinkling lights in the black ceiling. Two spotlights come on, and, searching the room, found us.

She looked surprised. The dance was not due till later, but now was the perfect time. I smiled at her.

Into the darkness came the disembodied voice of Barry White, '*We got it together, didn't we*?' At the sound of his low smooth guffaw, Lana smiled at me. Her beautiful forgiving eyes twinkled. And suddenly I was exhilarated. I loved her so much I felt my chest expand.

'Love you,' she mouthed.

When the vibrating haunting sound came, she moved her feet into position. The keys of a piano tinkled and Rihanna's unmistakable, silky voice cut through the dark, 'Shine bright like a diamond.'

Inside the spotlights, I curled one hand around her delicate little one while my other went to rest lightly on the small of her back. Then I was whirling her away and we were dancing our first dance. Our movements were so perfectly matched that the place became still. Not one person moved.

I knew we looked good together, but under the spotlights perhaps we looked special. I looked into Lana's eyes and got into the spirit of the dance, and the rest of the world dissolved. *This is you and me, girl. Just us.* She twisted her hips quickly from side to side, once, twice, thrice, then allowed her body to fall towards me.

I caught her and raising her high into the air held her aloft. Our eyes locked. The moment became magic. The notes held, shimmered. I returned her to the ground and we executed the large graceful circles we had practiced under the tutelage of Plazaola. I held her hand high above her head and twirled her fast as if she was a long corkscrew. While she was still spinning I caught her and wrapping my arms around her kissed her. It was long and deep and full of something that had never been there before. Then the music was over, and as if released, the spectators came alive and broke into applause. Even they could not deny the beauty of the moment.

She turned startled eyes towards them, and my eyes scanned the faces for Billie. I found her at the edge. She stood unsmiling, her hands resolutely clasped in front of her. I nodded at her. She understood immediately and started walking towards us. Three spotlights simultaneously hit the stage and found Rhianna. She was clapping. True to form the celebrity mad crowd gasped with pleasure and surprise.

'Yeah, it's me,' the star said and laughed. She held her arm out in our direction. 'I dropped in to congratulate the new couple. Give a hand, everybody, to Mr. and Mrs. Blake Law Barrington.'

I smiled politely and swung my eyes down to Lana. She had her hand clasped over her mouth with delight. This was a surprise for her too. Everybody clapped and cheered. I curled my arm around her waist and looked at her indulgently, proudly. Let them all see: there is nothing, nothing they can do to hurt us. She is my responsibility. My property.

'Thank you,' Rihanna shouted into the mic. 'Shall we get this party on the road?'

'Yeah,' the guests replied.

'I don't think I heard that.'

'Yeah,' came the louder, more definite reply back.

Dancers surrounded her and began gyrating. She started her next number, *Don't Stop The Music.*

Billie was standing beside us. I let go of Lana, and she looked up at me and smiled gratefully. Billie linked the fingers of her right hand through Lana's, and, gently kissing her cheek, led her away.

One of the security guys came up to me while I was watching the girls leave. I inclined my head slightly and listened while he explained that Victoria had used the invitation card meant for Lady Phelim. The anger returned to my limbs. When Lana was swallowed by the throng, I took my mobile out and called Brian. They were in the music room of the west wing.

I went across the lawn to the house. A man in a bouncer's suit and a Bluetooth in his ear stood at the door. When he saw me approach he held open the door. Brian and another man were standing on either side of a sofa, and Victoria was sitting down on it calmly waiting for me. One leg was curled under her and the other was swinging slightly. When she saw me she smiled insolently.

'You refused to invite me. So I invited myself.'

I looked at the table. Brian had laid the four blades on it. I looked at her hand. There were some remnants of sticking tape left on it. She had been intending to slash Lana. The surge of anger in my body is frightening. It is like the shrill screaming of a peacock. It startles and electrifies me. But my eyes return to her, genteel. I never give my enemies the satisfaction of rousing any emotion in me. And I wasn't going to start with her.

'I wanted to give her a present,' she explained pleasantly.

I tore my eyes away from the gleaming blades. I was so angry I wanted to strangle her with my bare hands. 'You're going to prison,' I said harshly.

She giggled. 'No, I'm not.'

I looked at her, perplexed, hunting for clues. Was she pretending to be crazy?

'Let's make a run for it. Is the car ready?'

'Are you fucking mad?' I growled.

'Help me, Blake. Don't let them take me away from you. They want to shrink my heart,' she whispered suddenly, her expression oddly vacant and yet her voice was bordering on hysteria.

I had seen that expression before. The unsightly memory of when I had last set eyes on her came back. Just for an instant that look had flashed across her face, but I had not wanted to believe it.

The mistake was mine. I had become soft. Even at work I didn't immediately go for the jugular. What had been interesting, even thrilling had grown into a sham for me. Sometimes, when I had the upper hand, when my opponent had not even seen my advantage, I had pulled back and compromised.

I went closer, shocked by the state she was in. I could not feel her soul, her personality. As if she was gone and there was this empty creature watching me. But as I got closer her eyes suddenly glittered and for a second something else flashed across her face, dark, oppressed, torn, but that too vanished. I realized then: she was dangerous in a way I had never imagined.

She was criminally insane.

I became still. I was in some way responsible, but I found it almost impossible to stay in the same room as her, let alone show compassion. I never wanted to see her again. I began to turn away from her, but she flew off the chair and landed with a thud at my feet, clung tightly to my leg like a monkey. I looked down at her, both startled and repulsed.

'I saw you first. She's not having you,' she snarled like a wild animal.

I experienced the irresistible desire to kick her in the ribs. To hear them crack. But she then said something that stopped me cold.

'We are both ugly,' she croaked. There was no joy in her eyes. She was crumpled and dwarfed by her surroundings, a creature made deplorable by her poisonous hate.

And suddenly my spectacular anger dissipated. She was right. We were both ugly. The only beautiful things in my life were Lana and the child she had created inside her body. I looked again at Victoria and tried to remember her when we were first engaged. Nothing in my life sang or danced, but certain little things dropped into the gray picture. Her sneering at the crockery, grumbling at the wine, sulky in a red coat and hunting boots, a miserable fashion worship, and an existence of being preoccupied, yet apparently doing nothing.

Lana changed all that.

I looked up to Brian. It took them a few minutes to pull her away from my leg.

She was screaming abuse and insults as I walked out of the room. It was far, far more serious that I had thought. I stepped outside into the evening air and taking my phone out of my pocket scrolled down my address book. All the lanterns were being lit and from the marquee came the sound of music and celebrating.

Victoria's father answered. His voice was surprised.

To my AWESOME readers,

As a writer it was always my intention to engage with my readers and keep them immersed in my characters. As such I am truly humbled by your continued support for the billionaire banker series, and particularly by your love for both Lana and Blake. With your feedback in mind, there will be one final installment to the Lana and Blake story. It will be available around early August as a free download for a month. Hope you enjoy it.

I'd also like to take this opportunity to humbly thank every amazing reader who went out of her way to leave precious reviews for any of my books. To show my deep appreciation I am running a raffle. Leave your review at the place where you purchased this book before the 29th of June 2014. Then let me know here: georgialecarre@gmail.com. And get put into the pot to win **USD100.00.**

Until we meet again, chase your most secret dream and... lick it ☺

41107729R00184

Made in the USA
Middletown, DE
03 March 2017